SILVER MOON

BY

RICHARD TERRAIN

BLACKNESS.

Pink Floyd's "Dark Side of the Moon (Brain Damage)" plays as WHITE TITLES appear over black. As the song crescendos at the FIRST chorus, SUNLIGHT flares over the lunar horizon and a crescent sliver of THE MOON is illuminated- huge, filling the screen from top to bottom. We're in space, circling around from the dark side until a HUGE FULL MOON fills the screen with whiteness- TITLES continue as we pull back from the moon, into the earth's atmosphere, through CLOUDS, until we reveal

PARIS AT NIGHT

We come to rest on an ancient, vaguely wolf-like GARGOYLE high atop a gothic cathedral in the Latin Quarter- a maze of narrow, twisting streets- desolate at this late hour. Clouds move over the moon. End TITLES. The song fades. A THUNDER CRACK. Rain drops spatter on the church's metal roof. Water trickles out of the gargoyle's mouth. We follow the STREAM OF WATER down to street level where it falls onto

A YOUNG COUPLE

wobbling down the street, sharing a bottle of wine. They open an umbrella and stand underneath it, smooching and giggling. We follow the STREAM OF WATER from their umbrella to the street, where it swirls into drain holes in the MANHOLE COVER that they're standing on. Suddenly...

CLANG!! The manhole cover pushes up under their feet. He flinches- bites down on her lip, drawing blood. She yelps.

CLANG!! The cover thrusts up again. They lose their balance, fall to the ground- the wine bottle smashes. The manhole cover flips off its hole. Horrified, they scramble from it. Then, out of it comes...

TERRENCE McDERMOTT

a fiftyish college professor in a turtleneck and old tweed jacket, clutching a well-worn leather shoulder bag and gasping for breath. He's balding, with longish grey hair and intense eyes. He climbs out of the hole, replaces the cover and dashes off desperately through the rain, looking back over his shoulder as he disappears into a narrow alley.

The couple watch him go, befuddled. She touches her hand to her lip and looks at the blood. She slaps her boyfriend upside the head.

                    GIRL
                  Idiot!

The guy shrugs. Then...

BAM!! The manhole cover explodes off the hole, sails twenty feet into the air and clatters to the ground some distance away. We cut to the couple's horrified reactions as they watch something emerge from the hole.

ON A NEARBY STREET

Terrence, running, hears the couple's horrible SCREAMS echo through the twisting streets. He comes to A STONE STAIRWAY and hurries down it, four steps at a time. At the bottom he turns right and arrives at a star shaped five-way intersection.

A low, muffled growl stops him in his tracks. He stands in the rain, panting, looking around at the dark maze of streets, trying to pinpoint the source of the sound.

                    TERRENCE
    (American accent- to himself)
  Where are you, you sick bastard...

A TAXI appears a block away. He waves his arms and calls out in a very good French accent.

                    TERRENCE

    Taxi! Ici, s'il vous plait!

It turns and drives towards him. He starts off towards it. He glances over his shoulder- sees nothing. He's twenty feet from the taxi. He smiles. Then-

He's jerked violently downward into A STORM DRAIN. He screams. Some monstrous force pulls him down, his bones crushing as his body is forced through the too-small drain.

The CABBY gets out and runs up to the drain, where TERRENCE'S thrashing upper body is quickly disappearing into the hole. Horrible growls and sounds of ripping flesh emanate from the sewer. BLOOD spurts through the grate. Terrence reaches up to the cabby, SCREAMING for help.

                    TERRENCE
          My God! Help! Au securs!

The terror stricken cabby shakes his head and starts backing up. Terrence lunges forth and grabs the cabby's leg. The cabby screams and tries to get loose. He falls to the ground and is dragged towards the hole. He grabs the bumper of his cab and strains to pull himself away, kicking at TERRENCE'S hand with his free foot.

LIGHTS come on in an adjacent building. A MAN in pyjamas runs out into the rain. The cabby loses his grip on the bumper and he and Terrence are jerked closer to the sewer but the man grabs the cabby's hand and pulls. Some OTHER RESIDENTS gather on the sidewalks. A police car SIREN approaches.

Something gives and the man in pyjamas falls backwards into a puddle. The small crowd looks down and sees TERRENCE, pulled free from the hole, moaning semi-consciously. We move down his body, past the bleeding stumps where his legs used to be, and follow the BLOOD as it swirls into EDDIES of rain water and flows into the BLACKNESS of the storm drain.

cut to:

A FIERCE BULL

charges through the matador's red *muletta*, snorting blood. The CROWD goes wild. We're in a bull fight arena, under the blazing Spanish sun.

The camera dollies past cheering SPANIARDS and finds a small group of AMERICAN STUDENTS, early twenties.

                    GORD
       Man. I can't believe I paid good
       money to watch a guy in tight pants
                 kill a cow.

                   SHERRY
        Disgusting. This makes American
           Gladiators look highbrow.

The camera settles on ANDY MCDERMOTT, 22, as he joins the crowd in a rousing cheer, waving a bottle of wine with native gusto. He's good looking in a scrappy sort of way, with shoulder length brown hair, grungy plaid shirt, khakis, and glasses.

                    ANDY
                 Whoo! Ole!
              (to his friends)
    Man, you guys are losers! This is
    poetry! Death in the afternoon, a
    tragic dance of man and beast, just
    like Hemingway said. God, Spain is
    it! These people know how to live.

                   SHERRY
     I still say we should've gone to
                    Paris.

                    ANDY
    Paris!? Ug! If I wanted to be in an
      overpriced, overrated city full of
        obnoxious assholes I would've
        stayed in New York! Please!

    Another friend, MIKE, joins them.

                    GORD
         Where've you been? Beatin' off in
                your sombrero again?

MIKE swats Steve in the head
playfully and grabs the wine from
ANDY. He hands him a crumpled
telegram.

                    MIKE
         McDermott, your dad sent this to
           the pensioner. Supposed to be
                      urgent.

                    ANDY
                  (concerned)
                What's it about?

                    MIKE
                  (defensive)
                I didn't read it.

ANDY takes the telegram. MIKE leans
in close to Sherrie and whispers
the gossip.

                    MIKE
        His uncle is in the hospital.

ANDY reads the message. His face
falls. For a SECOND, he's silent.
His friends see something's wrong.

                    GORD
        Hey, man. You okay? What is it?

ANDY grabs the wine away from MIKE
and takes a long swig. IN THE
BULLRING- the matador plunges his
sword between the bull's shoulder
blades and makes the kill.

cut to:

INT. PARIS HOSPITAL EMERGENCY WARD
- EARLY EVENING

BLOOD splatters on white paper.
Pull back to see a CHEF with a cut
finger standing at the admitting
counter, dripping blood on a form.

The uptight Parisian NURSE scolds him and pulls out a new form.

ANDY, lugging his back pack, trudges through the sliding glass doors marked "St. Severin Hospital". Bleary eyed, hung over, burdened by a heavy backpack and carrying the crumpled telegram, he approaches ANOTHER NURSE at the counter.

                    ANDY
    Um, excuse me... hello...

A STOUT WOMAN with a POODLE charges in front of ANDY and launches into a loud French argument with the NURSE over the hospital's "human's only" admission policy.

                    WOMAN
                   (French)
  Pitou needs a real doctor! He's
            melancholy!

                    ANDY
            Hey, wait a minute...

ANDY tries to push his way back in, but the shrill little dog yaps at him. ANDY grabs his aching "hangover head" in agony. The bleeding chef walks away, dripping, leaving the other NURSE free. ANDY approaches her. She has her head down in some paperwork.

                    ANDY
         Pardon... Excusez moi. 'Allo.

Without looking up, she holds up a "please wait" finger. ANDY sighs. The poodle yaps at him again. He winces and tries to get the NURSE's attention.

                    ANDY
                 (to NURSE)
              Umm...

She raises her finger sharply and glares at him. She goes back to her paperwork. ANDY starts chatting politely with her, pretending she's responding.

                    ANDY
So, you ever been to Spain? You'd love it. It's friendly, sunny, cheap... And you'd be the only raving bitch there instead of just one in the crowd up here.

MARCEL BOULARD, a short middle aged COP in a rumpled coat approaches. He taps ANDY on the shoulder.

                    MARCEL
        Andrew Mc-dair-*mo*?

                    ANDY
     That's Mc*Dermott*, but yeah.

MARCEL flashes his badge.

MARCEL
Detective Boulard. We've been expecting you. This is Inspector LEDUC.

LEDUC, in his fifties, taller, heavy set, droopy moustache, nods gruffly and starts towards the elevator, motioning for them to follow.

MARCEL (cont'd)
He's in charge but, uh, between you and me, my English is better. (they hurry to catch up with LEDUC) This way... So you're from New York eh? I love those Hill Street Blues...

ANDY
Right. Listen, my uncle, it's not serious is it? Did he eat some bad snails? Slip on the bidet? What?

They step into the elevator as LEDUC holds the door open. MARCEL and LEDUC trade uneasy glances. LEDUC sighs.

          LEDUC
          Merde.

          MARCEL
          He says-

          ANDY
   Yeah okay. My French isn't _that_
          bad.

INT. HOSPITAL ROOM

TERRENCE lies comatose under a clear plastic oxygen tent. An ORDERLY changes the dressing on his bloody stumps. A NURSE fiddles with the vast array of bleeping, burbling, sucking, life support machinery.

ANDY, dumb struck, watches from a few paces away. MARCEL, pad in hand, asks him questions. LEDUC stays in the background, listening and studying ANDY intently.

                    ANDY
                  Jesus...

                   MARCEL
          How well did, er, <u>do</u> you know him?

                    ANDY
           Not too well. He taught at the
          Sorbonne, right? Dad always calls
          him his "hippie brother". Did some
          work with Timothy Leary I think,
          and- Is he... is he going to die?

                   MARCEL
           No. The doctors say the machines
          should keep him going a long time.
          But basically he is, how you say, a
                    legume.

ANDY

Legume? You mean, a vegetable?

MARCEL

Vegetable, right. My mistake. It seems he was attacked by a maniac, maybe two or three maniacs, just after midnight. yesterday. They fled into the tunnels beneath Paris, that's all we know...

ANDY

What do you mean, maniacs?

MARCEL

Well, here's what I think happened. A chemistry professor goes to a bad part of town late at night. Why? Perhaps he's making a few francs on the side. The psychedelic drug market is big these days. He gets mixed up with a bad crowd and, like they say, if you lie with dogs, you get fleas.

                    ANDY
    Yeah, well, these fleas must have
      teeth like fuckin' chain saws.

BEEP BEEP! Something's wrong with
uncle TERRENCE'S machinery. The IV
bottle is sputtering and bubbling,
the EKG monitor is flashing. The
orderlies snap into action and pull
the curtain shut, waving "no
problem" to ANDY and MARCEL. MARCEL
leads ANDY awa y, trying to calm
him down.

                   MARCEL
Maybe we should go now. You must be
  very tired. We'll call if any new-

                    ANDY
I can't believe this. Why don't you
go down in the tunnels and find the
goddamn... animals that attacked my
                   uncle?

MARCEL
ANDY, it's not so easy. There are hundreds of kilometres of tunnels under Paris. It's a whole other city, crawling with drug addicts, lunatics, SKINHEADs... It's no man's land.

ANDY's about to protest when LEDUC steps in and hands him uncle TERRENCE'S leather bag.

LEDUC
Here.

MARCEL
Your uncle was carrying this. The keys to his apartment are in there. I talked to his assistant, Madame Flocquet. You'll be staying there a while?

ANDY
Yeah. I guess so.
(they walk him to the elevator)

Did he say anything? Before the
coma?

                    MARCEL
Just the name of this hospital, St.
Severin. He repeated it a few times
then he lost consciousness.

                    ANDY
Why would he pick this one?

                    MARCEL
I don't know. There were others
much closer. He was religious?

                    ANDY
Not that I know.

                    MARCEL
Well, when you're about to pop off,
what have you got to lose? Thanks
for your help.

ANDY's dumbfounded at MARCEL's lack
of tact. The elevator doors start

to close. LEDUC nods "good-bye". MARCEL leans in and sneaks in one last comment.

               MARCEL
     And remember ANDY, let's be careful
          out there. Heh-heh...Ouch!

The elevator doors knock him on the head as they close. ANDY shakes his head.

               ANDY
            (to himself)
     Inspector Clouseau, on the case.
                Great.

cut to:

EXT. TERRENCE'S APARTMENT BUILDING - NIGHT

ANDY opens the gate of this beautiful 19th century building and walks through THE COURTYARD to the

main entrance. A POODLE yaps at
him. The dog is in the open doorway
of the Concierge's apartment, which
opens into the courtyard. The nosy
concierge, MAD AME CHRETIEN calls
the dog, LULU, back in and shuts
the door.

ANDY enters the dark LOBBY, finds
the timed auto shut-off light
switch and turns it on. He boards
the old fashioned wire cage
elevator and presses the button for
#4. McDermott. The elevator ascends
painstakingly slowly. ANDY resigns
himself to waiting, thumbs through
his uncle's date book.

ANDY turns to the day Uncle
Terrence was attacked. A circled,
cryptic entry at the bottom of the
page reads "Meet CLAUDE, Medusa-
11:00". ANDY wrinkles his brow. At
this SECOND, the light goes out.

ANDY ascends the rest of the way in darkness. The doors open on the fourth floor. He gets out and finds his way to the apartment. He tries a key in the lock. It won't turn. He jiggles it. No luck. He goes through this with two more keys, grumbling under his breath. Finally, he finds the right one. He pushes the door open and gasps.

He's face to face with a scary TRIBAL MASK hanging in the entrance way. It startles him for a SECOND.

                  ANDY
     This must be the place.

INT. TERRENCE'S APARTMENT

ANDY walks in and sets down his bags. A gun COCKS. A young woman's voice screams at him in French.

                    YOUNG WOMAN
                    (in French)
          Who are you!? What do you want!?

He turns to see SERAFINE, a beautiful young woman, around 22, casually dressed and aiming a pistol at his head. He drops the shoulder bag and reaches for the ceiling.

                        ANDY
            Don't shoot! Jesus...uh...Je
          m'appelle ANDY. McDermott. Je suis
                    le... um, shit...

It dawns on her. She drops the gun to her side, embarrassed.

                      SERAFINE
                    (in English)
            Oh fuck, you are his nephew...

                        ANDY
          Yeah, that's the word. And <u>you</u> are?

SERAFINE
SERAFINE Flocquet. I work for your uncle.

ANDY
You? You're Madame Flocquet? I pictured a fat lady with an apron, not- I don't know- La Femme Nikita.

SERAFINE puts the gun away in a drawer.

SERAFINE
It sounded like someone picking the lock. After what happened, I guess I am a little nervous.

She lights a cigarette.

ANDY
Sure. I can follow that.

SERAFINE

It's a fucking nightmare, isn't it?

ANDY

Yeah. True. The COPs weren't much help either. Their theory is he was moonlighting as a drug dealer or something. Make sense to you?

SERAFINE

Police. They have their head in their asshole and they still can't find shit.

ANDY

Well put. So, what exactly has uncle Terrence been up to lately?

As he speaks, he scans the apartment. It's cluttered with an overwhelming assortment of anthropological oddities from around the globe, medieval illustrations, molecular models, and an artsy periodic table that's been used as a dart board.

                    SERAFINE
          He's doing a book with Professor
          Roussel, about medieval chemistry.
           I was just transcribing his notes
            onto the computer and - oh shit!

She races out of the room. ANDY follows after her.

INT. TERRENCE'S STUDY

She runs in and finds the computer locked up. She smacks it a few times, clicks the mouse, taps the keyboard. No response.

                    SERAFINE
              Salots! Shitfucker!

                    ANDY
        (reacts to her loose grasp of
              American slang)
                    What?

                  SERAFINE
    If you leave it for more than a few
      minutes it locks up. Now I must
      reboot and type a dozen fucking
      passwords. He was security crazy.

She flicks a switch on the back of
the computer, rebooting it. ANDY
pauses to look at some nearby
photos of his uncle.

                    ANDY
    I still can't get over it. The COPs
      said it was a "maniac", but he
      looked like, I don't know, like
        he'd gone through a combine
         harvester or... something.

SERAFINE gets kind of emotional at
the thought…

                    SERAFINE
            They wouldn't let me see him.
          Family only. I told them, Terry was
             almost like a father to me, you
                            know?

ANDY reacts to her use of the informal "Terry"...

                      ANDY
           Depends. Was "Terry" a father like
           Ward Cleaver or a father like Woody
                           Allen?

A beat. She grasps his meaning. She's offended. She starts typing on the computer, giving him the cold shoulder.

                    SERAFINE
            You must not have known him very
                well. He's not like that.

                      ANDY
             Hey, Sorry if I was out of line.

SERAFINE

You were. I have work to do. The publisher wants the transcripts by Monday. Go. Make yourself at home.

ANDY

Fine. My mistake. You know, I'm gonna be a writer myself someday.

SERAFINE

Uh-huh. Good for you.

ANDY sees he's sunk. He heads for the door, but something on the wall catches his eye. A small flyer on the bulletin board with a big drawing of Medusa. He takes it down.

ANDY

Medusa... What's this? some kind of club?

SERAFINE

It's nothing. A stupid party. Not really a night club, it's, uh..

ANDY

Like an underground club?

SERAFINE

Yes. It's a bad place. Weird people. Strange things go on.

ANDY

And who's CLAUDE?

SERAFINE looks at him hard, questioning.

ANDY

I looked through my uncle's date book. Writer's curiosity.

She points to a paperback on the desk. It's French, with a psychedelic cover depicting a man, half King Louis XIV, half witch doctor. The title, (in French) "History Inside Out - Psychic Illumination Through the Ages" by Dr. CLAUDE Roussel. A picture on the back shows an academic looking CLAUDE in a tweed jacket, with gray hair.

                    SERAFINE
        Professor CLAUDE Rousel. The one
         your uncle was working with. He
            teaches cultural history.

                     ANDY
        In an underground club? I'd like to
                    see that.

He shoves the book in his back pocket. SERAFINE's emphatic.

                    SERAFINE
         I'm serious. There's nothing for
          you down there. It's dangerous.

                    ANDY
     Come on. I'm from New York - the
     "shoot me" state. Don't wait up.

He starts for the door; she spins
him around by the sleeve.

                  SERAFINE
            (suddenly quite angry)
     What good can you do? Why are you
           being so fucking stupid?

                    ANDY
             (getting fired up)
     Maybe I didn't know him like you
       did. But he's my uncle. And I owe
     it to him to get some answers. It's
       a quest like, uh, Hemingway, the
     Old Man and The Sea. Except instead
     of an old man I'm a young man, and
     instead of the sea, it's a bunch of
     tunnels under Paris. And instead of
       a big fish it's... who knows?
     That's what I'm going to find out.
               Au revoir.

He walks out of the office. She calls after him.

                    SERAFINE
           You're a fucking lunatic!

The front door slams. She looks after him, incredulous.

                    SERAFINE
                    (French)
            God damned Americans.

cut to:

EXT. RUE D'ENFER - NIGHT

A MEDUSA HEAD is carved in the stone above the doorway of a crumbling old facade in a rundown Parisian neighborhood. ANDY tries the front door. It's locked. There's no sounds or signs of life.

                        ANDY
                    (to himself)
                  Some party.

ANDY starts off, then pauses as three PARTY GOERS approach the door. They're "modern-primitives"- tribal tattoos, pierced noses, and weird beaded hair. One fishes a key from the Medusa's mouth, opens the door, and lets the group in.

ANDY slips in behind them. One GUY in the group looks ANDY over and mutters something in French to his friends. They snigger amongst themselves and walk to a door across the foyer. ANDY follows, a few paces behind, through the door, down some stairs, into

A DILAPIDATED BASEMENT

 Lit with a few candles. They walk past an old boiler, through another door, into

A NARROW STONE SPIRAL STAIRCASE

They proceed down the ancient stairway, also lit only by the occasional candle placed on the steps. They reach the bottom of the steps and enter a dark, drippy stone tunnel, still lit by candles. Some rats scurry away through the puddles under ANDY's feet.

Candles lead the way through the maze of intersecting tunnels. Some graffiti scratched in the wall catches ANDY's eye: "Jean Philippe 1803". He pauses to look at it for and loses the group ahead of him. He follows the candles on his own, turning right, left, and left again. A loud, muffled bass beat gets louder. He rounds the corner into

THE WILD UNDERGROUND PARTY SPACE

In an open cavern, lit with torches and strobe lights. Two hundred people are gyrating to eerie techno-tribal dance music. It's a weird crowd, mostly young modern primitive pierced and grungy RAVERS, many wearing Day-Glo tribal face paint. Clusters of sullen, militant SKINHEADS hang around the periphery.

An attractive, blissed-out WAIF approaches ANDY with a paintbrush and a jar of day glo- face paint and a brush. She goes to paint ANDY's face. He stops her.

                    ANDY
          That's alright. I'll be a cowboy.

She smiles and pushes his hand down. He shrugs and lets her paint two-day glow red stripes on his cheeks.

                  ANDY
         Alright. Fine...
       (with mock enthusiasm)
   Ooh. I can feel it tingling.

ANDY sniffs and makes a face- the paint has a weird smell.

             ANDY (cont'd)
 Phew. What's in this stuff, liquid plumber?
   (he pulls the book out of his pocket and shows her CLAUDE's picture)
  Do you know this guy? CLAUDE?

                  WAIF
  Ah oui, le professeur. La bas.

She points to a dark alcove off the main cavern. ANDY nods and starts off. We move in on a leather clad young man leaning against the wall, watching ANDY go. This is GASTON DUFAUX, a self-styled Parisian thug, who seems to be cultivating a sort of "Mic key Rourke" look. He takes a drag from his cigarette and we see he's missing two fingers.

ANDY makes his way through the crowd. People are dancing with wild abandon, and many carry torches. A SKINNY GUY IN A DIAPER and a paper mache skull mask runs through the crowd, ranting and spraying fluorescent silly string. He does a weird dance around ANDY and jabbers at him in French.

                    ANDY
     Uh, lemme get back to ya on that.

ANDY approaches the side room and peers in. A small group of young people are listening intently to CLAUDE; whose back is to us. He's expounding about something in a solemn tone.

                    CLAUDE
               (French, to group)
     ...How ironic. A man who dedicated
      his life to opening the doors of
      the mind now lies trapped behind
      them. Locked behind a door without
                    a key.

We follow ANDY as he steps around the crowd and sees CLAUDE's face. He looks older than in the photo- he's in his late fifties, with white hair and intense eyes.

                     ANDY
               Excusez moi, I...

CLAUDE notices the book in ANDY's hand. He speaks fluent English.

CLAUDE
I'm sorry my friend, I'm not signing books right now. There's been a tragedy.

ANDY
I know. I'm ANDY McDermott. TERRENCE'S nephew.

CLAUDE is taken by surprise.

CLAUDE
My God, I'm sorry. But how did you find your way down here? Wait, let's go talk...

He excuses himself from his "flock" and leads ANDY to a quiet corner of the room. The kids disperse, several looking sympathetically at ANDY.

CLAUDE
It's horrible. Terrence was one of the most brilliant men I've known.

                    ANDY
   Yeah, well, why did he hang out
   here? The COPs said it's dangerous-

                    CLAUDE
    The COPs. It's their backward laws
    that force all this underground in
    the FIRST place, endangering people
      whose only crime is pushing the
    limits of perception, exploring new
         states of psychic awareness.

They're suddenly doused with Day-Glo silly string as the jabbering idiot in the diaper pops in to deliver a rant at them.

                 GUY IN DIAPER
                    (French)
     The moon is **bleeding**! Prepare for
              the downpour!

He ducks back out. ANDY picks the silly string out of his hair.

ANDY

Psychic awareness. Right.

CLAUDE

You think it's silly. But do you realize that young man is actually in a deep sleep?

ANDY

What?

CLAUDE

He's on a new drug called ZBH, or "Daydream". It allows the user to be fully alert and mobile while he's dreaming. He is literally conscious and unconscious at the same time.

ANDY

Yeah well, that's like really groovy and everything, but who hacked my uncle's legs off?

CLAUDE frowns. He looks grave.

CLAUDE
ANDY...

ANDY
Yeah?

CLAUDE
Terrence and I came down here to do serious work. For centuries these tunnels have been home to subcultures mainstream society would not tolerate.

He gestures to the main cavern, where people are far gone into various states... some in a trance, some gyrating lustily to the eerily hypnotic music. We intercut with these images as CLAUDE speaks.

CLAUDE (cont'd)
These people carry on traditions dating back to pagan times- the ancient quest for expanded consciousness. At the same time,

they're pioneering a chemical revolution, powerful state-of-the-art compounds... But you know what I mean....
(he gestures to ANDY's face paint)
A year ago who would have dreamed of topically applied hallucinogens like TMD? Except Terry of course...

ANDY's eyes widen with comprehension. He touches his face.

ANDY
What!? Hallucinogen? Oh shit...

He rubs the face paint off with his shirt sleeve.

CLAUDE
You didn't know? But then why did you... well, don't worry. It's relatively mild.

                    ANDY
 Yeah, well if I claw my face off,
just pack it in ice, okay? Jesus...
  the COPs were probably right. My
uncle was messed up with a bunch of
fry brains and they went berserk on
                    him.

CLAUDE lowers his voice. He looks
grim.

                   CLAUDE
No... We stumbled on something else
down here ANDY. Something horrible,
almost unbelievable. But very real.
  It's been going on for centuries,
though most people wouldn't believe
       it, or wouldn't want to...

ANDY's somewhere between spooked
and incredulous. He glances at the
book in his hand.

                    ANDY
        Wait a SECOND, are you like the
           Steven King of France or
                 something...

                SERAFINE (O.S.)
                    ANDY!

ANDY turns and sees SERAFINE run up
to him. She looks worried.

                    ANDY
         So you came after all. Just in
         time, it's getting interesting.

                  SERAFINE
        You must get out of here. It's not
                    safe.

She grabs him by the arm. He
resists.

                    ANDY
                Not you too-

                    CLAUDE
            (checks his watch)
My God! SERAFINE's right. It's time
        to go. We'll talk soon.

                   SERAFINE
          Bon nuit CLAUDE.
            (to ANDY)
          Come on.

CLAUDE dashes off. SERAFINE drags
ANDY into the main cavern.

                    ANDY
      Hey, chill out a SECOND!

She leads him across the cavern
towards the entrance. ANDY stops
short and pulls away from her. It's
not easy- she has a strong grip.

                    ANDY
Alright, hold on. I'm not gonna get
 dragged around like some kid in a

shopping mall. I want you to answer some questions.

SERAFINE sees something over ANDY's shoulder.

                SERAFINE
Merde. I knew I shouldn't have come here.

ANDY turns to see GASTON approaching. He leers at SERAFINE.

                GASTON
                (French)
SERAFINE, mon cher. I hear your boss looks great in cut-offs.

                SERAFINE
                (French)
Get the fuck away from me, GASTON.

                    GASTON
                   (French)
FIRST you tell me where the ADM is,
                     eh?

He puts his hand on her shoulder.
ANDY notices the missing fingers.

                   SERAFINE
                   (French)
                  Fuck you.

She shoves his hand away and pulls
ANDY past him. GASTON grabs her and
spins her around. This time ANDY
grabs GASTON's hand and pulls it
off her. He holds up GASTON's three
fingered hand and glares at him.

                    ANDY
Well, this explains the two fingers
 they found in Liberace's asshole.

GASTON jerks his hand away. He stabs his finger in ANDY's chest.

                    GASTON
    In Paris we have an expression for
        people like you: Enculé
                 d'Americain.

                    ANDY
      Yeah? In New York we got an
      expression too. Goes like this...

CRACK! ANDY hauls off and belts GASTON in the jaw as hard as he can. But GASTON doesn't even lose his footing. He sneers with rage and hits ANDY with a vicious combination. His glasses fly off as he reels into the crowd, knocking a few people into a group of nearby SKINHEADS. The SKINHEADs erupt into randomly directed violence- a full-fledged BRAWL breaks out. It's chaos.

On the floor, ANDY squirms away from the SKINHEADs and retrieves his glasses. He hears SERAFINE call his name. He gets up amidst the mayhem and sees SERAFINE being carried away by the crowd.

ANDY

SERAFINE!

Someone knocks into ANDY and he falls to the ground. He gets back on his feet- SERAFINE's nowhere in sight. He pushes his way through the crowd, looking for her. He catches sight of her white dress in a distant corner. It's there for a SECOND and then gone again - apparently into a tunnel. He runs over to it.

ANDY peers into THE TUNNEL, which houses some old pipes. It fades quickly into darkness. He grabs a kerosene torch from the wall and runs into the tunnel. About a hundred yards in he passes an ALCOVE.

He leans in with his torch and peers around. The cave like room is empty but something catches ANDY's eye. Scratched into the stone wall, amidst various graffiti, is A PENTAGRAM. It looks to be centuries old.

ANDY's transfixed by it. The sound of his own breathing suddenly becomes deafening and his vision begins to distort: the textures of the stone wall begin to churn and crawl, and the flames from his torch melt into different hues. The pentagram glows an d seems to grow out of the wall...

The hallucinatory flash is over as fast as it began. Panting, stunned,

ANDY shakes it off. He wipes his face, checking for traces of paint. He tries to reassure himself.

                  ANDY
            Whoa. C'mon.

A woman's SCREAM echoes through the tunnels. He runs towards it.

                  ANDY
            SERAFINE!?

Another scream- anguished, tortured. ANDY runs faster. He arrives at an intersection with another tunnel, turns the corner and finds...

A decrepit old WINO hogging a bottle from his warty HAG companion, provoking her to scream like she just lost her only son. They look up at ANDY. The hag shuts up. They fix ANDY with an odd stare.

                    ANDY
     Sorry...I, uh, did you see a GIRL,
     la femme, um, avec, la dress blanc?

They just stare at him. Spooked, he walks past them. They follow him with their creepy stare as he continues into the tunnel, which slopes downhill.

He comes to an old stairway leading down into darkness. WATER pours out of a hole in the ceiling. The steps are severely eroded and slick with flowing water and moss. ANDY sees something. It's SERAFINE'S SHOE, laying on a landing a few yards down the stairs. He leans in further, loses his footing and slips.

                    ANDY
              Ahh! Son of a bitch!

He shoots down the stairs on his back, past the shoe which lies at the mouth of an intersecting tunnel. His glasses come off. The torch goes out. He stops at the bottom of the stairs on a gravel surface.

He winces a bit as he sits up. It's too dark to make much out. He feels around the gravel, finds his GLASSES - they're shattered. He scowls. He stands up and walks ahead, feeling his way along the slick wall, peering into the darkness.

                    ANDY
              SERAFINE!?

The echo sounds different- like he's in a larger space. The echo decays into a familiar low RUMBLE.

A reflection of light appears in a puddle on the floor. The light gets brighter until ANDY sees the subway tracks at his feet. The rumble gets suddenly louder as

A METRO TRAIN

barrels around the corner, flooding the tunnel with light and closing on ANDY fast.

                    ANDY
               Oh shit!

He turns and runs for THE STAIRWAY. He skids on the gravel and overshoots it. He scrambles back and up into it just as THE TRAIN whooshes past.

ANDY scurries a few feet up the slick steps, using a rusty pipe for a handhold. As he looks back at the SPARKING, RUSHING TRAIN WHEELS, his heart pounding in his head, he has another HALLUCINATORY-FLASH: the sparks explode into streaking patterns of colour and light.

It passes quickly. The train goes by and its rumble fades. ANDY squeezes his temples and takes a deep breath. Before he finishes exhaling, an UNEARTHLY HOWL echoes through the tunnels. The howl literally takes his breath away- he's frozen there, eyes w ide, not breathing for a long moment.

Quietly, carefully, he makes his way back up the dark, wet stairs. He comes to the landing, picks up SERAFINE's shoe, and steps into the INTERSECTING TUNNEL. He squints into the darkness. Without his glasses, ANDY'S POV is a bit blurry. He walks into the tunnel. Another HOWL. ANDY swallows hard.

                    ANDY
              Jesus Christ...

He hurries along. WATER DRIPS from the tunnel ceiling, down the walls, onto the cobblestone floor, flowing into rivulets around ANDY's feet and joining a stream that flows ahead of him, disappearing into the blackness ahead. He approaches another inter section. He stumbles over something.

He looks down and makes out a GIRL'S BARE LEG lying in a puddle in the dark intersecting tunnel. He follows the leg up with his eyes- it's messily severed above the knee. He gasps.

He looks further into the tunnel and sees A PAIR OF GLOWING YELLOW EYES staring back at him out of the darkness. ANDY turns and runs.

With a horrible ROAR, the eyes lunge after him and turn the corner. As it gains on ANDY, we see the dim outline of the massive wolf-like beast.

ANDY dives for a SMALL CONDUIT, barely big enough for his body, and wriggles into it. Behind him the yellow eyes appear at the mouth of the conduit - the beast SNARLS but can't fit in. ANDY can see a dim light at the end of the conduit. He crawls along.

He emerges into ANOTHER TUNNEL. Some thirty yards away, light and street noise come through a GRATE on the ceiling of an antechamber beyond an iron gate. Relieved, ANDY starts off towards it. A SNARL stops him in his tracks. THE BEAST comes tearing around a corner fifty yards behind him.

ANDY breaks into a sprint towards the antechamber. He slips on the wet floor and lands in a puddle, drenching himself. The beast closes in.

ANDY gets up, runs into the antechamber and slams the iron gate shut. There's a rusty DEADBOLT lock on the gate, but no key. The beast is twenty-five yards away and closing fast - it's massive silhouette filling the diameter of the tunnel.

ANDY whips out his SWISS ARMY KNIFE, opens the screw driver and tries it in the old-fashioned keyhole- it doesn't work. The beast is twenty feet away. ANDY tries the can opener- no luck. Ten feet. ANDY jams the corkscrew into the hole. The beast leaps. The corkscrew turns. The DEADBOLT SLIDES.

SLAM!! The beast rams the gate, shaking the anteroom. But it holds. Flashes of CLAWS and TEETH thrash through the bars, but it's still too dark to make the beast out clearly. ANDY runs across the anteroom, grabs the steel sewer grate on the ceiling, an d hoists himself up.

Through the bars, he sees a BUSY BOULEVARD in the Pigalle (the "Times Square" of Paris). There's a COP a few paces away. ANDY screams to him.

                ANDY
        HELP! OFFICER!

ON THE BOULEVARD- Over the roar of traffic and midnight revellers, the COP can barely pinpoint ANDY's screams. He looks around, confused. He sees ANDY and angrily shakes his baton at him.

COP

(French)

Hey! You shouldn't be down there!

ANDY

FOR GOD'S SAKES, LET ME OUT!!

THE BEAST slams the gate, wrenching one of the iron bars loose- two more bars and it'll fit through. ANDY jumps down, picks up the loose bar. It's got a STAR SHAPED SPEAR TIP.

He rushes at the gate and jams the spear through the gate, aiming for the thrashing teeth and eyes in the darkness.

The beast ducks and the spear sinks a couple of inches into the BACK OF IT'S NECK and stops, apparently on bone. It recoils and ROARS with pain, shaking the spear free.

ON THE STREET- The COP raps the bars with his nightstick and peers into the dark anteroom.

           COP
       (in French)
You are not allowed down there!

IN THE ANTEROOM- The beast rams the gate- it's rage redoubled. ANDY jumps up and grabs the grate.

ANDY
GET ME THE FUCK OUT OF HERE!!

ON THE STREET

                        COP
                      (French)
"Fuck"? You think I don't know this
   word "fuck"? Is that how you talk
        to policemen in America?

Enraged, the COP runs to his car, muttering to himself. He opens the trunk and rummages around for something.

IN THE ANTEROOM- The beast knocks another bar off the gate. ANDY watches in horror as it rams even harder, loosening the NEXT BAR.

                       ANDY
                   (to the COP)
      FUCK! FUCK! FUCK! FUCK! FUCK!

ON THE STREET- The COP looks over at ANDY, incensed. He takes a crowbar from the trunk, runs back cussing in French, and struggles with the grate.

IN THE ANTEROOM- The NEXT BAR on the gate gives. The beast sticks its head through the gap and focuses its searing yellow eyes on ANDY. It rears back, ready to pounce...

THE GRATE- comes up. The COP grabs ANDY and pulls...

IN THE ANTEROOM- ANDY's legs dangle like bait. The beast lunges, teeth and claws bared.

ON THE STREET- ANDY screams as a bus roars by. The COP pulls him up and out. ANDY's right pants leg is torn open and he's bleeding from a GOUGE in his ankle.

                    COP
                (French)
Okay, what the hell are you up to?

                    ANDY

It bit me! My leg! Jesus, it's down
    there, shoot it! Shoot it for
           Christ's sakes!

He points frantically at the open
hole. The COP aims his flashlight
in the hole. It's empty. He looks
ANDY up and down.

                    COP
                 (French)
            Your passport.

Shaking, ANDY takes his passport
out of his pocket. The COP takes it
and Copies some information. ANDY
raves at him- a blur of English and
broken French.

                    ANDY
    There's something down there! A
     bear or something! A god damn
     monster! Beau coup teeth! Huge,

Grande, with yellow eyes, all this hair, it killed SERAFINE! My God...

                    COP
          You on drugs? Huh?

                    ANDY
               (he falters)
             No...I...

He looks disoriented, half-crazed. He definitely *seems* like he's on drugs. The COP shines his flashlight in ANDY's eyes- his PUPILS are like saucers.

ANDY'S POV

The COP's flashlight sparks another HALLUCINATORY FLASH. The COPs face melts like liquid, sounds swirl together, the garish neon signs of The Pigalle explode into streaking colours and we BURN INTO WHITE.

cut to:

EXT. TERRENCE'S APARTMENT BUILDING

The COP car pulls to a stop. The COP gets out, opens the back door, and pulls ANDY out. He pushes ANDY towards the building.

>   COP
>   (French)
>   Stay off the street.

The COP gets in the car and drives away. ANDY staggers to the gate in a daze and fumbles with the keys.

INT. APARTMENT BUILDING

ANDY walks up to the apartment door. Disoriented and shaking, he manages to open the door and walk in. He locks the door, and switches on the lights. He looks out the small PEEPHOLE. No sign of anyone or anything. He leans back against the door and rub s his hands across his face.

                    ANDY
          Oh god. Je suis seriously messed
                     up...

There's a DRIPPING sound coming from the kitchen. ANDY looks across the living room into the dark kitchen. The DRIP continues. He steps forward cautiously. Suddenly he feels something and looks down sharply.

UNCLE TERRENCE, bloody stumps and all, is clutching ANDY's legs and looking up at him desperately. He's trying to speak but can't seem to make a sound. Blood from his wounds soaks the WHITE BEAR RUG beneath them.

ANDY's terror struck, he tries to jump away but falls backwards to the floor. Terrence crawls up and gets close to ANDY's face. He croaks out two words in a rasp-

TERRENCE
Saint Severin...

INT. TERRENCE'S HOSPITAL ROOM - SAME TIME

The EKG monitor shows a FLATLINE. Alarms are BEEPING. TERRENCE'S body lies motionless under the oxygen tent. A DOCTOR and a NURSE rush to the bed. The NURSE rips the oxygen tent away and the doctor SLAMS his fists down on TERRENCE'S chest. The EKG show s a tentative blip. The doctor SLAMS again. An erratic heart beat starts back up on the EKG.

INT. TERRENCE'S APARTMENT - SAME TIME

ANDY lies passed out on the floor. Terrence is gone, and the rug is free from blood.
FADE TO BLACK.

INT. LEDUC'S OFFICE - DAY

MARCEL sits next to the patrol COP, PEROTIN, who rescued ANDY. They're hysterical with laughter. Even LEDUC, sitting behind his desk, is chuckling.

                LEDUC
               (French)
      What else did he say?

              PEROTIN
               (French)
     Yellow eyes...big teeth...
    (he can barely choke out the words
          between laughs)

> Covered with hair! Ha-ha-ha!

PEROTIN playfully growls at MARCEL. They laugh even harder.

> LEDUC
> (French)
> Okay PEROTIN. You can go.

PEROTIN nods, still laughing. MARCEL walks him to the door. Before he steps out, PEROTIN bares his teeth, growls again, and cracks up some more. MARCEL, laughing, claps him on the back and shuts the door- then he and LEDUC go instantly stone faced. They look at each other gravely.

> LEDUC
> (French)
> Well?

MARCEL
(grim)
Okay. So maybe you were right.

LEDUC
Hmmph. At least now there's one person around here who doesn't think I'm crazy.

LEDUC walks to a map of Paris on the wall covered with coloured push pins. He sticks a blue pin in it. He points to a green pin on another part of the map.

LEDUC
(French)
Twelve thirty-six a.m. here. Twelve forty a.m. here. There's two of them. At least.

MARCEL
Merde.

LEDUC looks at his calendar. Four days are circled in red ink.

                    LEDUC
                   (French)
       Two more nights in this lunar
                    cycle.

                    MARCEL
                Double merde.

LEDUC opens a tall cabinet, revealing a bookshelf stuffed with dusty tomes. He browses past dozens of titles about black magic and demonology.

                    LEDUC
       You better follow that McDermott
       kid. He's going to wind up like his
            uncle if he's not careful.

                    MARCEL
         Right. Little twerp thinks he's
                    Colombo.

LEDUC selects an old book and hands it to MARCEL.

                    LEDUC
       And do some research, will you?

MARCEL takes the book. He inspects the cover (it's in French)- "Werewolves through the Ages: from St. Severin to the present".

                    MARCEL
                   (confused)
               Saint Severin...

                    LEDUC
     You never heard the story of Saint
     Severin driving the werewolves from
                    Paris?

                    MARCEL
       You think that's what McDermott was
         raving about in the ambulance?

                    LEDUC
          What, you think everyone's as
                 ignorant as you?

MARCEL considers this.

                    MARCEL
                 Pretty much.

LEDUC grunts, exasperated.

                 MARCEL (cont'd)
          Inspector, you're not exactly
             typical. I mean c'mon...
                  (holds up book)
          This thing isn't sitting on a lot
                of coffee tables.

cut to:

INT. TERRENCE'S APT.- LATE MORNING

THE SAME OLD BOOK, sitting on the coffee table. The pages are stuffed with notepaper place markers, many covered with scribbling, and CHEMICAL NOTATION. In the background, on the floor, is ANDY- fast asleep and snoring where he collapsed the night before.

We hear a key in the lock. The door opens, smacking ANDY in the head once, twice.

                    ANDY
          Aoww! Hey! What the hell...?

He grabs the door so it can't hit him again. SERAFINE pokes her head around and sees him. She's surprised, relieved, elated. ANDY's reaction is more disoriented, stunned.

                  SERAFINE
             ANDY! Holy shit!

                    ANDY
             SERAFINE...?

She kneels beside him and helps him sit up.

                    SERAFINE
    Thank God! What a relief! I
    thought... After you disappeared...
     I couldn't find you... I thought
     all sorts of horrible things...

                     ANDY
Yeah... Ditto. I saw, er, I thought
I saw you get munched... like Uncle
                Terrence...

He looks over at the clean bear rug. ANDY rises to his feet groggily. He looks down at the rip in his pant leg. He feels the torn fabric, trying to remember.

                    SERAFINE
     What happened? Did you cut
                yourself?

                    ANDY
Um... sort of... Maybe... It's all
kind of blurry. We met at the club,
then... Damn, that was some weird
                    shit.

He goes over to the window and parts the curtains. It's a brilliant sunny day.

                  SERAFINE
That was fucking stupid, going down
 there. You could have been killed.
 I tried to warn you, But you don't
    listen. Just like your uncle.

ANDY's only half listening. He opens the window, and inhales deeply. Across the court yard, a MATRONLY WOMAN leans out a window, hanging her laundry. In the courtyard, Lulu the obnoxious poodle YAPS at another resident, and Madame Chretien calls her ba ck. ANDY's head is clearing. His mood lifting.

                    SERAFINE (cont'd)
          You have to be a hero. All
          Americans think they are cowboys.

                    ANDY
              (leaning out window)
          I was an Indian, actually. Man,
          that damn psycho paint...! If
          that's supposed to be mild, I don't
          want to know about medium.
              (he looks at the woman and smiles,
              the sun on his face. To himself:)
          The planet earth. It's good to be
          back.

                    SERAFINE
          So... you feel okay now?

He turns around and smiles at her.

                    ANDY
Yeah. Actually, I feel fan-fucking-
                    tastic.

SERAFINE laughs. She hasn't heard
this expression before. He
approaches her.

                  SERAFINE
          Fan-fucking-tastic?

                    ANDY
   Hey, what more could I want? I
   survived my FIRST and last
   hallucinogenic hell ride, and
   neither of us is dead. I'd say I
   feel almost as great as you look.

He makes a grab for her, and she
pushes him away.

                  SERAFINE
            Hey! Calm down.

He jumps up on the sofa, unable to contain his energy.

                    ANDY
    Come on SERAFINE. Let's go out.
    Show me the real Paris, the part
    that isn't overpriced and overrun
           with German tourists.

                  SERAFINE
    Go to Jim Morrison's grave at Pere
       Lachaise. It's overrun with
    American tourists. I have to work.

                    ANDY
    I know! Let's go hock loogies off
           the Eiffel Tower!

She digs in her pockets and hands him some coins.

                  SERAFINE
    Here. You go. "Hock some loogies"
              for me.

She turns and heads off to the office. He runs in front of her and blocks her path.

                    ANDY
What about food? Even beautiful women have to eat. It's true. I read it. Please? A half an hour?
            (pause. He sees she's tempted)
                  My treat?
        (she's smiling. He resorts to
                    begging)
Pleez! Don't make go out there alone again! I'm begging you!

                  SERAFINE
Okay. But I'm back in half an hour.

ANDY claps his hands together in triumph and scrambles to hold open the door for her.

                  SERAFINE
        What about your glasses?

                    ANDY
        It's okay. I can see fine.

She gestures to his filthy clothes.

                  SERAFINE
         Don't you want to change?

                    ANDY
       Man! Our FIRST date and already
       you're trying to get me to *change*!
          You French women work quick!

She smiles and pushes him back in the apartment.

CUT TO:

EXT. PARIS BOULEVARD- DAY

JERRY LEWIS

on a TV screen, dubbed with a zany French voice, undergoes a radical physical transformation in "The

Nutty Professor". Pull back to reveal ANDY and SERAFINE watching this scene on a dozen or so TV's in a store window display. Several PARISIAN PEDESTRIA NS watch Jerry with reverence.

     ANDY
  Now *this* is Paris!

On screen, the Nutty Professor's alter ego, "Buddy Love" launches into his swinging version of "That Old Black Magic". To this accompaniment, we cut the following-

PARIS MONTAGE:

- AT A BRASSERIE: ANDY is about to escort SERAFINE into the trendy eatery, but she stops him at the door and points to the menu, or more specifically the prices. He makes a horrified face, and they move on.

- IN A BOULANGERIE: SERAFINE buys cheese, ANDY buys meats- the counterman shows ANDY how big a slice off the pate loaf he's about to cut. ANDY nods "yes". The counterman cuts it and offers the slice. ANDY shakes his head "no" and points to the much larger remainder of the loaf.

- AT AN OUTDOOR MARKET: Detective MARCEL, wearing a lame "disguise" (new wave sunglasses ala "Diva"), watches ANDY and SERAFINE shop from a distance.

- IN A PATISSERIE: ANDY points to a large baguette, says something suggestive and winks boastfully at SERAFINE. She gives him a "yeah, right" look and points at a small breadstick.

- IN A WINE STORE: ANDY looks at each bottle closely, then "tests" it by shaking vigorously. SERAFINE's amused. The owner's baffled.

- ON THE RIGHT BANK: Arms full of groceries, ANDY and SERAFINE pass the row of outdoor pet stores near the river. ANDY looks longingly at the live ducks in their cages. SERAFINE pulls him along. MUSIC fades out.

EXT. ILE SAINT LOUIS - SUNSET

ANDY and SERAFINE sit on the river bank facing a magnificent Paris vista. SERAFINE unpacks the food.

SERAFINE

Shit! You bought enough pate for a fucking army!

ANDY

So tell me, exactly which truck driver did you study English with?
She laughs and pushes him playfully.

ANDY

Like I should talk. Monsieur foot-in-the-mouth. I'm really sorry about that whole Woody Allen thing...

SERAFINE

So's Woody Allen.
(ANDY laughs. She starts uncorking the wine.)
No, your uncle really helped me. I was sort of messed up for a while. Wasting my time just partying and... just stupid shit. He kind of

woke me up, gave me a job, got me taking classes.
(she uncorks the wine and fills their plastic cups)
You know, he and CLAUDE, their work is controversial, but they're serious about it. Totally dedicated.

ANDY

That's what counts. If you're not passionate about it, don't waste your time. That's why I quit college... Plus I'm a lazy bastard.
(CONTINUED...)

ANDY (cont'd)

(They raise their cups.
ANDY taps his forehead.)
Wait, I know this... A votre sante.

SERAFINE

A la votre.

They "clink" and drink. He notices her KEYCHAIN lying on the ground.

It's a miniature replica of Rodin's famous sculpture, "The Kiss". He picks it up.

                    ANDY
          This looks familiar...

                  SERAFINE
       Ahh, Rodin. Mmm! He's the fuc-
             (she catches herself
              and laughs)
     I mean, he's the best. You must go
      to the Rodin sculpture garden, in
       the huitieme, it's so beautiful.

She gestures across the river. ANDY looks at the gorgeous panorama.

                    ANDY
     Yeah, I gotta admit, you French are
           pretty good at beautiful.

He looks at SERAFINE. She looks back at him. He holds up "The Kiss"

                    ANDY
        I bet you're pretty good at this
                    too.

She smiles playfully.

                  SERAFINE
            What, sculpting?

He shakes his head "no" and moves towards her. They kiss tenderly. They separate and share a deep, passionate look. They kiss again, hungrily, falling into a passionate embrace. They're really going for it. Her NAILS dig into his back. He pulls her bod y into his until they look like one form- just like Rodin's sculpture.

APPLAUSE and CHEERS break the moment. A TOURIST BOAT is gliding by on the Seine, it's ELDERLY PASSENGERS applauding the young couple. SERAFINE pulls away, blushing a little, and turns to the boat. ANDY doesn't even notice the boat. He's staring at Sera fine with a scary kind of intensity. She starts to say something but he starts kissing her again, cutting her off.

Suddenly he's out of control, pawing at her... It takes an effort for her to pull back from him.

                SERAFINE
        Hey, calm down a SECOND...

She looks into his eyes and freezes with fear. HIS STARE is terrifying, totally predatory, inhuman. Something's ignited in him. She pushes him away and shakes him.

                SERAFINE
        What's wrong with you!?

ANDY blinks and seems to come a couple of steps back to normality.

                    ANDY
      What? Aren't I a good kisser?
            What's the matter?

She fixes him with a heavy, suspicious stare. She glances down at his ankle, where the bottom of HIS WOUND is visible. She seems to understand something. She fumbles in her purse, takes out a compact mirror, and checks her face.

                  SERAFINE
    God, look at my lipstick. Look, I'm
     going to run into the bathroom at
     that cafe. Stay here and watch the
                stuff, okay?

She gets up and starts off. He looks after her.

                    ANDY

                 SERAFINE...

                  SERAFINE
         I'll be right back. Stay put.

She runs up the steps to street
level. ANDY watches her go. He
turns back to his glass of wine and
chugs it. He puts the bottle to his
lips and takes a long belt. He
picks up the big block of pate and
bites into it like a piece of cake.
He likes it. He takes another huge
bite. He looks after SERAFINE. He
gets up.

INT. CAFE

SERAFINE puts her "telecarte" into
the pay phone and dials. She looks
anxious, upset. We hear the phone
ringing at the other end. Behind
her, ANDY comes into the cafe. He
walks up to her, pissed off.

ANDY

Fixing your makeup with a phone, huh? Who the fuck are you calling?

SERAFINE

Professor Roussel. There's something wrong with you. I know it.

ANDY

Roussel? You mean CLAUDE? You're calling Dr. Demento so he can come paint my face again? Fuck that.

ANDY starts backing away.

SERAFINE

ANDY, stop! I think he can help you-
(CLAUDE picks up)

CLAUDE (V.O.)
Allo?

                    ANDY
What, you think you're gonna catch
fucking leprosy from me? Fuck that
shit! If I'm not good enough for
     you I'll find someone else!

He turns and storms out of the
cafe. SERAFINE's flustered.

                  SERAFINE
                   ANDY!

              CLAUDE (V.O.)
                 (French)
SERAFINE? Is that you? What's going
                on?

                  SERAFINE
                 (French)
  CLAUDE, it's ANDY, he's acting
  really weird, I think something
       happened last night...

               CLAUDE (V.O.)
     God, well don't let him go! Catch
                    him!

She drops the phone and runs out of
the cafe. On the sidewalk, she
looks in all directions. Nothing.
ANDY's gone.

                  SERAFINE
                    Fuck!

INT. CLAUDE'S OFFICE.- SAME TIME

CLAUDE's sitting at his desk, phone
to his ear. The room is stuffed
with books.

                   CLAUDE
              SERAFINE? Allo?

He hangs up. He strokes his chin
and furrows his brow, sinking deep
into thought.

cut to:

EXT. STREETS OF PARIS - NIGHT

Music cue: "Wolf Call" by Elvis Presley. ANDY pays for a crepe at one of the roadside stands, and eats it as he walks along the narrow sidewalk, still brooding about SERAFINE. He stops to gawk at the PRETTY GIRLS that pass by, and bumps into a young FR ENCH TOUGH with a ROTTWEILER.

          FRENCH TOUGH
        Idiot!

          ANDY
        Ah, bite me!

He glares at the tough and his growling dog. The dog suddenly shrinks back in fear and decides it's time to leave. He pulls his owner along. ANDY continues on his way. He ditches the half-finished crepe. That's not what he's hungry for.

ANDY comes upon a trendy little CAFE with several tables of diners eating in the open air. ANDY notices an attractive young blond sitting alone, thumbing through a "Let's Go" guide. This is AMY SINGLETON. ANDY approaches confidently.

                    ANDY
    Ahem. Did you know that, according
    to the "Let's Go" code of conduct,
      whenever two Americans meet in
      Paris, the one with the sexiest
         smile has to buy dinner?

AMY smiles. She is indeed sexy, with remarkable, sparkling BLUE EYES.

                    ANDY
    Damn! You win!... Waiter! Garcon!

He jumps into the seat across from her.

                    AMY
    Actually, I'm waiting for someone.

                    ANDY
    What a coincidence, I *am* someone!
              (sniffs)
    Mmm. Calvin Klein's Obsession. Now
              it's mine too.

She laughs. The waiter arrives to take their order. ANDY hands him the empty half bottle of wine from AMY's table.

                    ANDY
    Hi. Another, bigger bottle for this
      ravishing blue eyed Goddess and
      myself. And, avez vous le Steak
                  Tartar?

CUT TO:

INT. TERRENCE'S APARTMENT BUILDING HALLWAY - SAME TIME

SERAFINE unlocks the door and enters the apartment. She's stopped cold by what she sees. The place has been totally ransacked - drawers opened, shelves cleared, furniture overturned, the works. The window is open.

          SERAFINE
     Merde! Salots!

She walks across the room, kicking at the debris in her path. She stands in the middle of the mess, absolutely furious.

          SERAFINE
     Aaaaah!

EXT. STREET - CONTINUOUS

Across the street from the apartment building, GASTON pauses to light a cigarette. He hears SERAFINE's distant scream, looks towards the building, and walks away.

cut to:

EXT. CAFE - NIGHT

Three successive tables of upscale PARISIAN DINERS are gawking at something. At one table, Inspector MARCEL hides behind his menu, and shakes his head in disdain.

We follow their glances to ANDY, greedily licking the last bits of Steak Tartar off his plate. AMY giggles in amazement as she pours the last from the bottle of wine.

She's a bit drunk- enough to be amused by ANDY's antics.

                    AMY
         God. How can you eat like that?

                    ANDY
         It's all in the tongue. Another
                   bottle?

AMY laughs and nods "yes". JEAN-LUC, 25, a well-dressed, powerfully built Frenchman enters. He kisses AMY on both cheeks, all the while watching ANDY uneasily.

                    AMY
          JEAN-LUC. You're kinda late
                   sweetie.

                  JEAN-LUC
         I was busy. Is this a friend of
                    yours?

                    AMY
          Well, yeah, kinda', but-

                    ANDY
          We're so much more than friends.
          We're soul mates, sex slaves, pen
          pals, the whole nine yards. Well,
             nine yards is a slight
          exaggeration, but believe me, for a
          white boy, I got nothing to be
                  ashamed of.

     AMY laughs in mid gulp and wine
     comes through her nose. ANDY looks
     at JEAN-LUC, who is - of course -
     pretty steamed.

                    ANDY
           Hey, I'm kidding... It's a joke!
           Here, maybe if I say it in metric.

     JEAN-LUC grabs ANDY by the collar
     and pulls him to his feet.

                    JEAN-LUC
               Think you're smart, huh?

AMY tries to intervene.

                      AMY
               JEAN-LUC, don't be a jerk.

She tries to pull his hands off ANDY, but JEAN-LUC sends her reeling back with a firm shove.

                     ANDY
               Hey, look man, she-

JEAN-LUC brings his hand back and slaps ANDY in the mouth.

                    JEAN-LUC
               Shut up. Why are you Americans
                    always so loud?

                    ANDY
I don't know. Maybe it's so we can
drown out the sound of your mother
          fucking the navy?

JEAN-LUC takes a swing at ANDY. With amazing reflexes, he dodges it deftly. JEAN-LUC jabs- again ANDY avoids it easily. He smiles, impressed with himself. JEAN-LUC is incensed.
He goes for ANDY's throat, but ANDY catches him by the arm and, with **superhuman strength**, FLIPS him head over heels, through the air and - SMASH! - onto a nearby table.

ANDY casually leans past the semi-conscious JEAN-LUC and plucks a CHAMPAGNE BOTTLE out of its ice bucket. The WAITER is about to object, but thinks better of it. ANDY takes AMY by the arm, she grabs the RED WINE BOTTLE, and they start off away from the cafe.

                    AMY

          Wow. You know Kung Fu or something?

                    ANDY
                (amazed at himself)
              Yeah. Apparently.

In the background, MARCEL hurries to pay his tab and follow them. He slips on some of the broken glassware spilled by JEAN-LUC's fall, and almost goes for a tumble himself.

FURTHER DOWN THE STREET

AMY and ANDY walk together. She's still giddy.

                    AMY
            Ha ha. You were probably right
                  about his mom.

                    ANDY
            Hope I didn't hurt him too bad.

AMY

Who gives a shit? I've had it up to here with arrogant Frenchmen.

ANDY

Up to there? Really? I bet I could beat that.

AMY

Ha ha! Yeah right, white boy! Ha Ha ha.
(she hiccups)
I think maybe I drank too much.

ANDY

Ah. The mating call of the blonde. The night is young, the moon is bright, whataya feel like doing tonight?

AMY

I don't know... Surprise me.

He thinks a moment, then puts his arm around her and whispers in her ear. She squeals with delight.

                    AMY
        Are you kidding?! I LOVE Jim
                Morrison!!

Inspector MARCEL, who's eavesdropping from around a nearby corner, rolls his eyes to heaven. Oh brother. The Doors' "Backdoor Man" kicks loud as we

cut to:

EXT. PERE LACHAISE - NIGHT

MARCEL is hiding behind a grave, spying. His passion for police work has been reborn, judging from his rapt, totally absorbed stare. He's watching...

ANDY AND AMY

having extremely hot and primal sex on Jim Morrison's grave, lit by dozens of flickering candles people have "left for Jim". He pours red wine into their mouths. Sweat and wine drip off their naked bodies. The sex heats up to an intense, screaming climax. AMY squeals with ecstasy.

                      AMY
    My God! You're an <u>animal</u>!

But ANDY's still accelerating- transported to another plane. Sweat pours from his brow. His face contorts with each groan, but now it's hard to tell if it's from pleasure or pain. His body jerks violently and his skin suddenly blushes bright red. AMY winces.

                    AMY
        Ahh! Jesus! You're burning hot!
                What the hell-

                    ANDY
                  AHHHHHHH!

MARCEL is a little disconcerted.

                   MARCEL
             (French, to himself)
        Alright already, you passed the
             audition for God's sakes.

ANDY's skin literally glows red, turning his sweat to steam. He leaps off AMY and disappears into the sprawling cemetery, screaming in agony. AMY watches him go.

                    AMY
           Hey, where are you going!?

MARCEL starts off after ANDY, taking the wide route around AMY.

ANDY's scream echoes through the cemetery. AMY pulls her dress on.

                   AMY
              Creep.

ANDY

red hot (literally), weaves through the tombs, screaming. He comes to a small courtyard with an ORNATE FOUNTAIN. He dives into the brackish water. Clouds of steam rise off the water as he thrashes about under the marble goddess in the centre of the fountain.

                   AMY

  searches through the graveyard. She's got ANDY's clothes.

                    AMY
I don't know what's wrong with you,
 man, but I got your pants, so we
           better talk.

THE FOUNTAIN

ANDY's gurgling screams are changing, becoming less human. We catch glimpses of body parts as they surface from the churning froth- GROTESQUE, FLAILING LIMBS somewhere in mid-transformation between human and beast.

MARCEL

steps cautiously through the ancient, ornate tombs and mausoleums, listening to the distant splashing and sporadic inhuman screams. He draws his gun and loads a cartridge. Suddenly a horrible grunt and loud SMASH pierce the air. MARCEL wheels around an d smacks nose FIRST into a gravestone.

                    MARCEL
                    Merde!

                     AMY

in another part of the graveyard, stops in her tracks, listening. Another SMASH followed by crumbling, and rushing water.

                     AMY
                 (to herself)
He's gone psycho ballistic. This is bad.

AMY feels something and looks down. There's a stream of water flowing around her feet. She follows it towards its source and steps into

THE COURTYARD

The fountain has been smashed- the stone rim cracked into bits and the centre statue fallen to the ground. There's no sign of ANDY. AMY walks up to the fountain.

                    AMY
          Oh my God...

She notices something on the ground. It's the STONE GODDESS, smashed into several pieces. We hear a low growl. AMY looks up, terrified. She scans the GRAVES around the perimeter of the courtyard. She takes a few tentative steps backward.

Suddenly a MASSIVE TOMBSTONE is wrenched off its base (most of the ancient stone markers are eroded and crumbling- many already fallen over). It falls like a tree, revealing the familiar pair of piercing yellow eyes behind it, framed by the dim outline of a massive beast. AMY emits an odd, primitive whine.

                    AMY
                  Unnnhh...

She runs away from the beast, across the courtyard and disappears into the graves.

In the DENSE FOREST OF TALL TOMBSTONES, AMY zigs and zags through narrow spaces, barely wide enough for her slender body to fit through. The camera CRANES UP.

HIGH ANGLE

Thirty paces behind AMY, pairs of tombstones split apart like jungle vegetation, crashing thunderously to the ground. The unseen beast's path is slowed by the monuments, but still follows AMY.

AMY looks back as she runs. She sees the tops of tombstones fall behind her. She comes to a railing at the top of a fifteen-foot wall separating a LOWER LEVEL of the cemetery. She hangs over the edge and quietly drops.

She runs down a path comes to an intersection where six paths converge. She looks down each of them, but can't see the outer walls of the cemetery- just an endless landscape of graves. She sprints down a path and ducks behind A LARGE CRYPT.

Up on the higher level, the beast howls. She looks up and sees its silhouette sniffing the air, the full moon looming behind it. She looks up at the iron door on the crypt. Then she reaches into her purse...

THE BEAST'S POV

Its HEAVY BREATH dominates the soundtrack. It scans the sprawl of graves from its perch on the hill, sniffing. It locks it's stare on the large crypt. It sniffs again. With a growl, it leaps over the railing (we stay with its POV) and hits the ground running. It runs up a twisting path, closing in on THE CRYPT. It arrives at the back of the crypt and circles it, sniffing. It stops in front of the door.

THE BEAST'S EYES

Narrow and glow with intense predatory focus.

INSIDE THE CRYPT

We're looking at the door. CRASH! It flies open, revealing the snarling beast, backlit by the moon. It lunges in and stops.

THE BEAST'S POV

Scans back and forth- the crypt is empty. The beast sniffs again and growls with rage.

                    AMY

 somewhere else in the graveyard, sprays a long blast of perfume into another crypt, and sneaks into the endless maze of tombs. We hear the enraged beast smash into another crypt a hundred yards away.

AMY comes to ANOTHER FOUNTAIN and slips into the water, quietly rinsing herself.

THE BEAST'S POV

smashes into another crypt. Nothing's inside. It backs up and runs to another crypt. SMASH! Nothing. The growls grow more furious. It crashes down another door. Nothing.

AMY, dripping wet, pads down a row of ancient family mausoleums. She pauses as the beast lets loose a horrible howl and topples a monument some distance away. She tries the heavy iron door on a SMALL GOTHIC MAUSOLEUM. It opens. She slips inside.

IN THE MAUSOLEUM

AMY crouches under the small portal and STAIN GLASS WINDOW, which depicts the Virgin Mary. She struggles to quiet her breathing, and listens...

She hears only the trickling water from the nearby fountain. Then... some crackling twigs...then a SNIFF...another SNIFF, closer. Trembling, AMY quietly raises herself, peers out the portal and sees
MARCEL

Standing a few paces away, SNIFFING and trying to stem the flow from his bloody nose.

          MARCEL
     Merde...

AMY breathes a sigh of relief. Then-

THE BEAST springs out of the darkness behind MARCEL- a blur of eyes, claws, and teeth- and tackles him to the ground.

IN THE MAUSOLEUM

AMY drops down to the floor, huddled in terror. A GUN SHOT hits the STAIN GLASS above AMY's head, shattering the Holy Virgin. Another GUN SHOT followed by a ROAR OF PAIN from the beast. But the pained roar quickly becomes VICIOUS SNARLING again. There are no more shots, just horrible snarls, screams, and ripping flesh. BLOOD splatters through the portal and drips down AMY's face. She hunkers down. Then, the sound of steps going away, and at last...silence.

AMY waits. We hear only the fountain and another, closer DRIPPING. It's AMY's wet clothes, still dripping into A PUDDLE on the floor, which is dripping UNDER THE

IRON DOOR, into a small STREAM flowing on the otherwise dry STONE WALKWAY, away from the Mausoleum.

In the mausoleum, AMY listens a bit more. Satisfied the coast is clear, she quietly turns to the iron door, grasps the handle and slowly turns it. But before it clicks open-

RRRIIP!! The iron door is wrenched out of AMY's hand and
off its hinges, revealing

THE BEAST, up close and in clear view for the FIRST time- it's truly awesome- a huge leering mouth full of razor sharp teeth, a hulking body built like a wolf but as massive as a bear, and vaguely humanoid paws with big hook claws. There's a bloody FLESHWOUND in its right shoulder.

It snarls savagely at AMY. She chokes out a little cry. The beast lunges.

OUTSIDE THE MAUSOLEUM - HIGH ANGLE

The beast's powerful hind section sticks out of the mausoleum, kicking a bit as it rips into its prey. The graveyard sprawls endlessly under the big moon, which hangs low in the sky.

FADE TO BLACK.

EXT. TERRENCE'S APT. BUILDING COURTYARD - MORNING

We hear Lulu the poodle's bell jingling behind a bush. Madame Chretein pokes her head out her door and whistles for Lulu. The bell keeps jingling, but Lulu doesn't come. She calls its name.

It still won't come. She steps out into the courtyard in her bathrobe and walks towards the bush, calling for the dog, annoyed as its disobedience. She looks behind the bush and sees- A CROW picking at the scant remains of Lulu, ringing the collar bell with its beak. She SCREAMS.

INT. TERRENCE'S APT. - SAME TIME

ANDY wakes up in a cold sweat, naked on his Uncle's couch. The phone is ringing. He looks disoriented, confused. We hear Madame Chretien screaming in the background.

              ANDY

          Jesus...

He sits up to get the phone and becomes dizzy- he grabs his head. He reaches for the phone and winces- there's a crusted over FLESH WOUND on his right shoulder. He picks up the phone.

                    ANDY
                    Hello?

              SERAFINE (O.S.)
              (anxious, concerned)
              Are you okay?

                    ANDY
          No, I don't think so... I was
           having a nightmare. Wait a
                   SECOND...

              SERAFINE (O.S.)
         Where did you go last night? What
                  did you do?

                    ANDY
         I don't... I... I can't remember...

                    SERAFINE (O.S.)
          Listen, I'm coming over. Don't go
            anywhere. Stay right there.

She hangs up. ANDY is very confused. He sees the front door- it's ajar and the door frame has been splintered where the deadbolt sits. Stunned, he stands up, only to double over with a wave of nausea. He covers his mouth and runs stooped over to the bathroom.

He leans over the toilet and vomits. After a few heaves his body relaxes and he catches his breath. He opens his eyes and looks down in the bowl- horror and disbelief sweep over his face as he focuses on:

A HUMAN EYEBALL

staring back at him from the bloody water. The iris is a familiar shade of sparkling blue...

                    ANDY
            Oh no...no...

The doorbell rings. He leaps up, flushes the toilet and runs out of the bathroom, still naked, to find himself in full view of LEDUC and two UNIFORMED COPS standing in the open door. One of the COPs is examining the splintered door frame.

LEDUC looks to be in an even worse mood than usual. His English is rough, but firm.

                    LEDUC
            Get dressed.

cut to:

INT. POLICE MORGUE - MORNING

We're close on a metal body drawer. A TECHNICIAN pulls it open, revealing a severed human foot, nothing else.

LEDUC, ANDY, and the TECHNICIAN stand by the drawer in this dreary room. LEDUC never takes his eyes off ANDY's face.

          LEDUC
    You recognize her?

          ANDY
      What?!

LEDUC looks down, sees the foot, and barks at the TECHNICIAN.

          LEDUC
       (French)
  That's the wrong one!

The TECHNICIAN checks his clipboard and tries another drawer. It contains a rotting ARM. LEDUC curses under his breath. He and the TECHNICIAN start opening drawers at random, peeking in, then slamming them shut.

                    ANDY
                  (nervous)
       You, uh, you want to tell me what
                this is about?

LEDUC ignores him, continuing to open drawers. The TECHNICIAN appears to have found the right one at the far end.

                  TECHNICIAN
            Inspector! C'est le voici.

A little exasperated, LEDUC and ANDY go over to see what the TECHNICIAN has found. Once again,

LEDUC gives him the nod. He opens the drawer to reveal

AMY'S MANGLED CORPSE

It's badly lacerated. Parts of her throat and midriff are missing, and she has only one eye. ANDY gasps in horror.

                    LEDUC
          We know you were with her.

                    ANDY
              Oh shit... No...

                    LEDUC
            That's not all...
     (he reaches for another drawer
              above AMY's)
       MARCEL- Officer Boulard was
              following you.

                    ANDY
              Oh no... no....

He pulls open the drawer to reveal MARCEL'S MANGLED CORPSE. There's a gaping hole in his midsection.

                    LEDUC
          He was a good man. Now his wife is
                    a widow.

                    ANDY
                  (overcome)
          This is.. it's like a sick joke, I-

LEDUC grabs ANDY by the collar and slams him against the wall

                    LEDUC
           This is not a joke! Not a dream!
             These people are dead and--

TAP TAP... Through the small window in the door he sees CHIEF PICARD, his superior, trying to get his attention.

                    LEDUC
Merde... Wait here. When I return
you tell me about last night, huh?

                    ANDY
But.... I don't remember anything;
            I swear...

                    LEDUC
                  (sternly)
I leave these open. Maybe something
            comes back to you.

He leaves the room. The TECHNICIAN leaves too. ANDY's alone, staring at the corpses. Through the window, he can see LEDUC arguing loudly with his superior... ANDY tries to breathe deeply, calm down. He turns back to look at AMY's corpse. Suddenly, her eyes - well, her eye - snaps open and looks straight at him!

                    AMY

     Thanks for the lovely evening,
                  shithead!

                    ANDY

     Aaaaa! Jesus! This isn't happening.
     I'm still hallucinating. Shit!

ANDY storms around in a fit of
disbelief.

                    AMY

     You really know how to show a GIRL
          a good time, don't you?

OUTSIDE THE ROOM

LEDUC and the CHIEF have stopped
their argument briefly to watch
ANDY stomping around, gesturing
wildly. They resume their argument.

CHIEF
(French)
Okay. So he's weird. Maybe on drugs. Still, that's not-

LEDUC
I'm telling you. It's not drugs. It's something more. Someth-

CHIEF
Don't give me your black magic bullshit! Seven mutilations in forty-eight hours and all you find is a scrawny American boy? Do you have a motive?
(LEDUC hesitates)
Do you have a weapon? Or do you want me to believe he did it with his own two hands?

LEDUC
(exasperated)
I told you. These murders are not normal.

The CHIEF rolls his eyes, "here we go again" style. Meanwhile,

INSIDE THE ROOM

ANDY is still pacing the room madly.

                 AMY
Face it boyfriend. This *is* really happening.

                ANDY
No it isn't! You're *dead*!

MARCEL comes to life and peeks over the top of his drawer.

               MARCEL
I'm afraid she's not so lucky. She's undead. And so am I.

                ANDY
Aaaaa!!! Get the fuck away from me!

MARCEL

What are you so damn angry about?
Did somebody turn into a wild beast
and rip *your* intestines out? Huh?

AMY

I spent four years on Stairmaster
for this bod and you rip through it
like a pork chop. Thanks.

ANDY blinks hard. Every time he opens his eyes, MARCEL and AMY are still there, hideous as ever, staring at him.

ANDY

Okay... dead or undead... what do
you want from me?

AMY

A-*duh*... You're a werewolf. And we,
as your victims, have to walk the
earth until your curse is lifted.

                    ANDY

   Uh huh... And, supposing I believed
     that, what could I do about it?

                 AMY/MARCEL
                  (together)
              Kill yourself.

                    AMY
            It's the only way.

                   MARCEL
      It's not so hard. I used to think
     about it all the time. Maybe you
           should meet my wife.

ANDY buries his head in his hands.

OUTSIDE THE ROOM

                   CHIEF
           Enough. Cut him loose.

                    LEDUC
     I can't! At midnight tonight, he
        will kill again. It's crazy!

                    CHIEF
   Are you crazy? We have nothing. Let
    him go, then watch him. If you're
      right, you can pick him up at
     midnight. Or maybe he'll lead you
      to the others. Just let him go.

The CHIEF leaves. LEDUC scowls. He looks in at ANDY, still gesticulating wildly and talking to thin air. LEDUC re-enters the room and looks at ANDY bitterly.

                    LEDUC
            You're free to go.

ANDY looks from LEDUC to the drawers and back again.

                    ANDY
                    Me?

LEDUC gives him an angry stare.

cut to:

EXT. ILE DE LA CITE - DAY

ANDY walks past Notre Dame, flanked by MARCEL and AMY.

              MARCEL
Hanging is nice. Never goes out of style. What about hare-kare- a taste of the Orient? But no! You're in Paris! Try the Guillotine! There's one in the Louvre!

              AMY
I'd use pills. They're painless.

              MARCEL
Oh give me a break! He could use pills back in America! Why not get a little culture?

ANDY stops in his tracks- overwhelmed, desperate.

                ANDY
Look, I didn't mean to hurt anybody... God, I didn't mean to... to...

                AMY
Rip my face off? Hey, we all make mistakes. Hell, I didn't mean to sleep with you on the FIRST night, especially without a condom. But I did, and now I'm paying the price.

ANDY slumps over, beaten. AMY puts her arm around him. MARCEL pats him on the back. They start him walking along.

                MARCEL
Let's face it. It's a, how do you say... mother-fucker. But we're all

in it together. That's why we're trying to help you.

                AMY

              Exactly.

HOOOOONNNNK!! ANDY looks up to see a speeding bus about to flatten him. AMY and MARCEL have lead him into traffic. He jumps back and the bus just grazes him. Of course, it passes right through AMY and MARCEL. They're still standing there when it's gone.

              MARCEL
        Merde! Just missed!

                AMY
              (to ANDY)
    Uhh! Would you die already!

ANDY's adrenaline is pumping. There's still some fight in him.

                    ANDY
Fuck you! If I'm gonna kill myself
I'll do it when I'm good and ready!
         You can go to hell!

                   MARCEL
   No we can't. That's the problem.
   God knows it would beat hanging
            around with you!

ANDY socks MARCEL and breaks his jaw- off. It skitters off into the street. He punches him in the gut- SKLURCH! His fist gets stuck in the tangle of MARCEL's abdominal organs.

While ANDY tries to pull his hand free, AMY rears back and kicks him in the balls. He wrenches his hand loose and staggers back, clutching his groin.

                    ANDY
        Hey, you can't kick me! You're an
                  apparition!

                    AMY
        What, all of a sudden you got a
           degree in supernatural law?

MARCEL fits his jaw back into place.

                   MARCEL
         Call it the power of suggestion.

He socks ANDY in the mouth. ANDY shakes it off, rips MARCEL's arm off, bashes him in the face with it, then turns around and uses it to beat AMY over the head. Meanwhile...

IN AN UNMARKED POLICE CAR PARKED A HALF BLOCK AWAY

RENE and FRANCOIS, the two COPs who accompanied Le Duc to ANDY's apartment, watch ANDY whirl around the sidewalk, swinging wildly at the air, reacting to invisible blows, and cursing unseen enemies.

                RENE
              (French)
   You know, in his own way, he's
   probably happier than any of us.

FRANCOIS nods philosophically. Meanwhile, back in ANDY's reality...

MARCEL has got him in a full Nelson and AMY is punching him in the stomach. He bucks forward, wrenching both of MARCEL's arms off and slams them together onto AMY's head, knocking her down. ANDY waves MARCEL's arms in triumph.

                    ANDY
                   Ha-ha!

                    AMY
        Oh, big man. You can beat up a
        couple of cadavers. Well let me
      make something real clear, asshole.
        If you don't kill yourself, at
         midnight tonight you're gonna
        transform and murder innocent
                   people!

                   MARCEL
          What are you going to be,
      McDermott? A coward and a murderer?
        Or a man, with guts enough to do
                the right thing?
        The truth of this question hits
      home with ANDY. A heavy expression
      falls over his face, one of grave
      sadness, but also inner dignity. He
         breathes deeply and exhales.

                    ANDY
        Alright. Let me write a letter.

                    MARCEL
      Good man. Now can I have my arms
                     back?

cut to:

EXT. NEWS STAND - DAY

Music cue: Thelonius Monk's "Round Midnight". The NEWS STAND MAN hands ANDY some stamps. ANDY sticks them on a letter addressed to Mr. and Mrs. William McDermott. He starts walking away but a postcard in the display rack catches his eye- it's Rodin's " The Kiss". He looks at it sadly.

A MAILBOX

ANDY drops the letter in the box. He walks to a pay phone on the sidewalk. AMY and MARCEL lean on a nearby building, watching ANDY dial. TERRENCE'S answering machine picks up.

> TERRENCE'S machine (O.S.)
> (French)
> Hey. This is Terrence. Please leave a message at the beep...
> (CONTINUED...)

> TERRENCE'S MACHINE (CONT'd)
> (English)
> In other words, this is Terrence McDermott. Please leave a message.
> (it BEEPS)

> ANDY
> Hey, SERAFINE, I hope you're checking these. It's ANDY. So I guess you knew what was wrong with me yesterday. Unfortunately, it took me until today to realize it, and because of that two people are dead. If you *didn't* know, well,

shit, it's irrelevant now. I know what I have to do, but before I do it I just wanted to say... I don't know what would've happened with us, but I'm really glad I had the chance to know you even if it was only a couple of days and... I don't know... I probably wouldn't have the nerve to say this if I was gonna see you again, but I think if I had the chance to kiss you one more time I would've fallen totally in love with you.

INT. TERRENCE'S APT. - SAME TIME

The door opens, SERAFINE enters and runs to the machine.

          ANDY (On machine)
   Oh well... Bye SERAFINE.

SERAFINE snatches the phone off the receiver just as ANDY hangs up. She gets a dial tone. She's very upset.

                    SERAFINE
                    Merde!

ON THE SIDEWALK

AMY and MARCEL watch ANDY hang up in the phone booth. The emotion of the moment is getting to AMY.

                      AMY
          Geez, I feel bad for him. Maybe we
                should've told him abou-

                     MARCEL
          Are you crazy!? You know that's
          totally impractical. Besides, like
                  the Bible says...
              (he sticks his finger in her
                  empty eye socket)
              An eye for an eye...

AMY nods. ANDY exits the phone booth and approaches them. "Round Midnight" fades out.

					ANDY
				Let's do it.

cut to:

EXT. ESPLANADE - DAY

ANDY drains the last of a bottle of Jack Daniel's and wobbles along, totally smashed and a bit wistful, with AMY and MARCEL in tow.

					ANDY
			What the hell, lots of my heroes
			killed themselves. Hemingway, Van
			Gogh... um...Herve Villachaise...

					MARCEL
			But this is class kid, all the way.
					What a way to go.

                    AMY
You got style, babe. That's why I
went for you in the FIRST place.

WIDE SHOT

They're approaching the Eiffel tower.

                    ANDY
When they ask how I died, just tell
            'em... *Ei-ffel*.

THE COPS

sit in their car, watching ANDY buy his ticket and get into the elevator.

                  FRANCOIS
                  (French)
          Should we follow him up?

                    RENE
    Well, he's gotta come down some
    time. Fuck it, let's grab a bite.

                    FRANCOIS
            Good thinking.

cut to:

INT. PATISSERIE - DAY

It's a typical Parisian bakery, stuffed to the ceiling with an unbelievable array of the finest, most delectable pastries. RENE steps to the counter.

                    RENE
            Vous avez les doughnuts?

cut to:

EXT. EIFFEL TOWER OBSERVATION DECK - DAY

We're looking at the elevator doors. They open. ANDY strides out onto the deck, through the milling TOURISTS, flanked by MARCEL and AMY.

                ANDY
There's only one thing certain in life- each of us owes God a death.

Proud, determined, ANDY arrives at the six-foot wire mesh fence and quickly scales it. AMY and MARCEL follow. Nearby tourists are alarmed and a clamour of concern rises up. Those with camcorders jockey for position.

            ANDY (cont'd)
All we can do is make sure it's a good one.

ANDY gets over the fence and stands on the small ledge. AMY and MARCEL join him. The tourists gasp. ANDY glances down at THE PRECIPITOUS DROP. He turns suddenly pale.

          ANDY
    Shit. I feel sick.

         MARCEL
Don't worry. In a few SECONDs you won't feel a thing.

          ANDY
Puking on yourself in mid-air is not a good death.

          AMY
Look, the more you think about it, the harder it is.

         MARCEL
Just like sex with my wife.

                    AMY
          The key is don't look down.

                    MARCEL
          Also like sex with my wife.

                    AMY
                 (to MARCEL)
          Would you shut up?

ANDY looks woozy. Tourists are trying to dissuade him in Italian, Japanese, Icelandic, etc. MARCEL tries a new tack.

                    MARCEL
          Tell you what, we'll jump together.

                    AMY
              (picking up MARCEL's lead)
          Sure. We wouldn't ask you to do anything we wouldn't do. Now give me your hand...that's it...

AMY coaxes ANDY's hand off the fence. The crowd gasps. ANDY grits his teeth and focuses again.

                    AMY/MARCEL
        One... two... three... JUMP!

They jump, but ANDY stops short- GASTON is leaning over the fence and has ANDY by his shirt.

                      GASTON
        You're not getting off so easy.

AMY AND MARCEL

Plummet through the air. They look back at ANDY, annoyed.

                      MARCEL
        Merde! I can't believe this!

                    AMY
    You try to be a good sport, and
            look what happens.

SPLAT!! Their bodies split into several pieces and squirt out on the pavement into two radial patterns, each about ten feet in diameter. Repair will take a while this time.

              MARCEL'S HEAD
        Huh. Galileo was right.
               AMY'S HEAD
                  Who?

GASTON
has ANDY by the arm and is trying to pull up to "safety". The tourists cheer him on. ANDY is resisting.

                  GASTON
      Where's the ADM? Where did your
              uncle put it?

ANDY

Man, I don't know what the fuck you're talking about.

GASTON

Bullshit! Your uncle told you!

ANDY

My uncle's in a coma, you moron!

GASTON

Before the coma!

ANDY

He didn't tell me anything. All he said was Saint *Severin*...

ANDY swallows the word "Severin", remembering something as he speaks. Suddenly wheels are turning in his head.

GASTON

Saint Severin? The church? So you know all about the ADM!

>   (ANDY reacts to the
>   word "church?")
>   Where is it! Tell me! Tell me or
>   else!

                         ANDY
            Or else what? You'll <u>kill</u> me?

                        GASTON
           No. But I'll kill your fucking
                    GIRLfriend!

                         ANDY
             You'll never get the chance.

ANDY pulls backward as hard as he can, jerking GASTON off balance. He's trying to pull them both to their deaths, but GASTON grabs a STEEL POST with his free hand.

ANDY hangs below the ledge, pulling GASTON's arm down with all his new superhuman strength. But GASTON pulls back <u>just as hard</u>. ANDY sees

The STEEL POST start to bend. He looks into GASTON's FERAL STARE and understands...

                    ANDY
It was you! You son-of-a-bitch! You
            got my uncle!

The POST keeps bending- its welds won't hold long.

                    GASTON
Don't be an idiot! I'm not the only
    one. If I die, SERAFINE dies!

                    ANDY
     Bullshit! You're bluffing!

                    GASTON
What, you think CLAUDE hangs out
    underground cause he likes to
                dance?

This gives ANDY pause.

                    ANDY

                  CLAUDE...?

                   GASTON

            And you call _me_ a moron...

ANDY stops pulling. He looks uncertain- maybe GASTON is right... But then- SNAP! The post, which has bent all the way over into a "J" shape, snaps its weld. GASTON and ANDY plummet towards the ground nine hundred feet below. The tourists gasp.

Using the bent pole as a hook, GASTON snares a HORIZONTAL ANTENNA which sticks out of the tower about fifty feet under the observation deck. He stops short and dangles there, still gripping ANDY by the arm. The tourists CHEER. Meanwhile, nine hundred feet below...

RENE AND FRANCOIS

lean on their car, munching doughnuts. The tower looms behind them, and we can just make out the dangling figures at the top. RENE reaches into the paper doughnut bag and comes up short.

>					RENE
>				(French)
>		Oh! You ate the last jelly!

UP ON THE ANTENNA

GASTON's grip is firm. They'll have to climb up the iron cross beams to the observation deck.

>					GASTON
>		The ADM. Let's go.

>					ANDY
>		Yeah, okay. Just gimme a minute to freshen up.

cut to:

ON THE OBSERVATION DECK

ANDY and GASTON climb up onto the deck. The tourists applaud and cheer for GASTON- the "hero".

                TOURISTS
    Bravo! Magnifique! Wunderbah!

GASTON can't resist posing as the cameras flash- he sucks in his cheeks, purses his lips and does his best "Mickey Rourke". ANDY looks at him, incredulous.

                  ANDY
    I must be in Paris. Even the
        werewolves are poseurs.

cut to:

INT. TERRENCE'S APT. BUILDING

GASTON and ANDY endure the elevator ride together.

          ANDY
So, if you and the nutty professor are both werewolves, what do you want with drugs? You like seeing lots of pretty colours when you're tearing people's throats out?

          GASTON
If you know about the church, why ask such stupid questions?

They step out of the elevator and up to the apartment door. ANDY takes his key ring out and tries the lock. The key won't turn. ANDY jiggles it.

          ANDY
Damn...

He tries another key. It doesn't work. He jiggles it, rattling the door on its hinges.

            GASTON
        What's the problem?

            ANDY
    Hey, I'm new here, what do you
                want?

ANDY tries a third key. No good. More jiggling.

            GASTON
        Fucking cretin...

The fourth key works. ANDY pushes the door open. GASTON shoves him in roughly and steps in after him.

INT. TERRENCE'S APARTMENT

GASTON shuts the door behind him and walks over to ANDY, who scans the room nervously, unsure of his next move.

                    GASTON
          Where is it? Hurry up!

ANDY's eyes come to rest on the end table drawer, where SERAFINE had put the gun before... He advances toward it.

                    ANDY
                (patronizing)
          Okay, okay. I got your magic
     medicine right here, dog boy. Just-

GASTON grabs ANDY's hand before he opens the drawer.

                    GASTON
          Do you think I'm an idiot?

                    ANDY
            (beat...incredulous)
          Sure. Don't you?

He shoves ANDY away and opens the drawer... no gun. They hear a pistol COCK behind them.

                  SERAFINE
          Looking for this?

GASTON turns and sees SERAFINE aiming the gun at him. With incredible speed he leaps for the window as SERAFINE fires. BANG!! The bullet catches him in the arm as he dives through the glass. BANG!! She fires again and misses.

GASTON lands in the courtyard, three stories below, and runs off with a slight limp. BANG! BANG! SERAFINE fires blindly into the courtyard after him, overwrought with anger. ANDY puts a hand to her

arm, and she lowers the gun. They
embrace tightly, desperately.
SERAFINE can't keep from crying.
ANDY comforts her.

                    ANDY
          Hey, hey... shhh. It's okay now...
            La Femme Nikita strikes again.

He wipes away her tears and she
smiles at his joke.

                  SERAFINE
          ANDY, I thought... I heard your
          message and... thank God you're
                      alright.

She embraces him again, but ANDY
gently frees himself.

                    ANDY
          I'm not alright. We both know that.
          The only reason I'm here now is to
          warn you. You're still in danger.

GASTON told me that CLAUDE has got the curse too. He's a werewolf.

          SERAFINE

I know. He told me.

          ANDY

What?! He told you? When?

ANDY hears a familiar voice behind him.

          CLAUDE

Two weeks ago.

ANDY spins around to see CLAUDE standing by the hallway to TERRENCE'S office. ANDY reaches for the gun and points it at him.

          ANDY

You two faced bastards. I knew you were full of shit.

                    SERAFINE
                   ANDY! No!

She puts herself between CLAUDE and
the gun barrel. ANDY pushes her out
of the way.

                     ANDY
SERAFINE! Move! Don't you see, he's
   just after the drug, that ADM
stuff. He's using you to get to it,
   just like he used Uncle Terrence.

CLAUDE approaches ANDY, speaking
calmly.

                    CLAUDE
   You're exactly right, ANDY. I
   enlisted both SERAFINE and your
   uncle to obtain ADM. And now I'm
   counting on your assistance too.

                    ANDY
          Why the fuck would I do that?

                  SERAFINE
          Because, ANDY. It's a cure.

                    ANDY
                  A cure?

                   CLAUDE
         A cure. With ADM we can wipe out
           lycanthropy, the curse of the
                werewolf, forever.

ANDY is shocked, stunned, sceptical. He bluffs with the only card he's got.

                    ANDY
         Is that so? Maybe we should go to
         Saint Severin church and make sure,
                     huh?

CLAUDE's face changes. He's surprised.

            CLAUDE
 Ah, you've done your homework...
Excellent. Get your coat. Leave the
  gun with SERAFINE. She can keep
searching. We don't have much time.

ANDY and SERAFINE share a heavy look. He hands her the gun.

           SERAFINE
ANDY... I should never have let you
     go underground. I'm sorry...

             ANDY
       (shaking his head)
I had to be a damn Hemingway hero.
Well I'll tell ya, The Old Man and
the Sea didn't go through half this
               shit.

cut to:

EXT. SAINT SEVERIN CHURCH - EVENING

Sheets of rain crash down over this ancient gothic church. Sharing an umbrella, ANDY and CLAUDE walk inside.

INT. UNMARKED POLICE CAR

Parked across the street, RENE and FRANCOIS watch them enter the church. RENE talks into a cellular phone.

> RENE
> (French)
> He's going into Saint Severin church with Professor CLAUDE Roussel.

INT. LEDUC'S OFFICE - SAME TIME

                    LEDUC
                  (on phone)
        Really... Okay, keep checking in.

LEDUC hangs up and thinks a moment. He turns the page of the old book on his desk, revealing an old woodcut illustration of a policeman being attacked by a werewolf. He frowns.

INT. SAINT SEVERIN CHURCH - EVENING

An evening mass is in progress. The boys' choir fills the church with a solemn hymn. ANDY follows CLAUDE to a narrow staircase. An OLD WOMAN gives them the evil eye and crosses herself as they pass. CLAUDE and ANDY go up the stairs and arrive at a balcony under a magnificent wall of ancient STAINED GLASS. One of the panels catches ANDY's eye.

ANDY

Whoa...

THE PANEL shows a weird medieval ritual- a man draining blood from another man's neck into a goblet. ANOTHER PANEL features a pentagram. ANOTHER PANEL shows a huge werewolf eating a monk under a frowning sun. All the transcriptions are in Latin. CLAUDE signals ANDY to follow him.

CLAUDE

The panels that concern us are over here.
(he directs ANDY to a group of panels)
I'll translate the Latin.

A PANEL shows a different werewolf, tied down, being stabbed in the heart by a knight under a frowning moon.

                    CLAUDE
     "Then Simon did slay the demon
      spirit, the same as had made him
                   unclean,"

THE NEXT PANEL- the knight now
holds the beast's heart aloft,
impaled on his dagger. Where the
beast was, a man lies bleeding in
the background.

                    CLAUDE (cont'd)
     "and Simon did cut out the heart of
      the beast which once dead, regained
              the shape of a man"

THE NEXT PANEL shows the beast's
heart on a platter. The Hero is
sitting at a table, cutting into
the heart with a knife, as if he's
about to eat it.

                    CLAUDE (CONT'D)
        "Simon ate of the heart of the
        beast and his soul was cleansed."
                 (he turns to ANDY)
        These pictures are not just myth,
        ANDY. The scholars of the day used
        them to record facts and enlighten
        the public. This is the medieval
                version of a newspaper.

                          ANDY
                       (sceptical)
        Yeah, well what if it's the Weekly
                    World News...

                          AMY
            No. It's all true, ANDY...

Startled, ANDY turns to see AMY and MARCEL, a little worse for wear, standing behind them.

                    AMY (cont'd)
I mean, if by some miracle you can
find the werewolf that bit you, and
then manage to eat its heart, the
curse is lifted. I was gonna tell
 you but MARCEL wouldn't let me.

                    MARCEL
   Oh sure, it was all mean old
MARCEL's idea. Give me a break! We
didn't tell you because it's a wild
    goose chase! Not to mention
         disgusting. Look...

MARCEL reaches into his own chest cavity, rips out his own slimy purple heart, and thrusts it in ANDY's face.

                MARCEL (cont'd)
  A little Grey Poupon and then Bon
               appetite, eh?

ANDY grimaces and turns back to CLAUDE.

                    CLAUDE
                   (to AMY)
        I don't believe we've been
                  introduced.

                     ANDY
        What?...Oh, right, you can see
           these guys too. Jesus...
              (he rolls his eyes)

                     AMY
       (smiles and extends her hand)
           AMY. Nice to meet you.

CLAUDE shakes her hand- SQUISH. Some sort of body fluid oozes out of AMY's hand. CLAUDE frowns and discreetly wipes his hand with a handkerchief. MARCEL smiles and extends his hand.

                    MARCEL
                    MARCEL.
       (CLAUDE smiles politely, declining
           MARCEL's rotting hand)

> My wife has all your books.

CLAUDE nods "thank you". ANDY's had enough.

                ANDY
Great. Later on we'll have to get together for cocktails. Right now I kinda have to hurry before I grow a lot of hair and eat people.
           (to CLAUDE)
Say this heart thing works. What's it got to do with ADM?

              CLAUDE
It's chemistry, ANDY. Nothing more. Mutated antigens concentrated in the heart of the infector unlock a vaccine-like chain reaction in the infected. There were not many bio-chemists working in the twelfth century, but with today's technology it's possible to synthesize any chemical imaginable.

When I discovered this ancient cure I knew who to go to.

ANDY

Uncle Terrence.

CLAUDE

Yes. I was able to decode the old texts and give Terrence the specifications. It took a lot of trial and error, but finally he got it: Adenine Di-Methyl oxide. ADM. I call it ADAM. But just before he was attacked, he hid it...

ANDY

Because GASTON was after it.

CLAUDE

Yes, that sociopath. He's given himself over to the evil of lycanthropy. To him, ADAM is just a threat to the terror he holds over others. To us, it's salvation.

MARCEL

Yeah, well I don't know much about chemistry, but even if this stuff works, you better find it by midnight. Otherwise it's-

ANDY

Yeah, I know. Back to the Eiffel Tower.
(to CLAUDE)
And what about you?

CLAUDE

Believe me, I won't go through another night of that hell. I have my contingency plan right here.

He removes a WHITE PILL from his coat pocket and holds it up.

CLAUDE (Cont'd)
Sodium cyanide.

The CHURCH BELLS ring. The group listens tensely as the solemn bells sound eight times.

                    ANDY
Eight o'clock. Shit. You'd think my
  uncle would have left a clue, a
          note, something...

                    CLAUDE
 That's what SERAFINE is searching
for. Without much luck, I'm afraid.
  If only we could speak with him.
   But alas, he's off in another
        realm, close to death.

The wheels in ANDY's head are turning. He looks over at AMY and MARCEL. He smiles. He's got an idea.

                    MARCEL
    ANDY, please. Don't smile like
      that. You're scaring me.

CUT TO:

INT. HOSPITAL - NIGHT

ANDY and SERAFINE walk down the corridor of the Terminal Ward. ANDY looks determined. SERAFINE looks upset.

          SERAFINE
What makes you so sure this will work?

          ANDY
I told you. He already tried to contact me once. If you saw his face. He was desperate to tell me something. I owe him this.

          SERAFINE
I don't know...

          ANDY

Listen, either he wastes away as a pathetic vegetable or he can give what's left of his life to save hundreds of potential victims. He's a McDermott. I know what his choice would be.

SERAFINE
I suppose you're right. But I still don't like it.

They stop at the door to TERRENCE'S room.

ANDY
Fine. You don't have to watch. Stay out here and stand guard.

She nods. ANDY goes into

TERRENCE'S HOSPITAL ROOM

The lights are off. ANDY approaches TERRENCE'S oxygen tent. In the dim light, he can barely make out

Terrence through the plastic, lying motionless, barely making an impression under the sheets. He looks at the body wistfully and surveys the array of machinery that's keeping him "alive". Most of the machines are plugged into a TRANSFORMER BOX on the floor.

ANDY
Hey. We meet again... Look, I know you understand what I'm about to do here. I think. But I hope you forgive me anyway.

ANDY takes a deep breath. He leans down to the transformer and opens the safety cover, and flips the power switch. All the machines power down.

Suddenly the old man in the bed sits up, gasping, and clawing at the walls of the oxygen tent. Oh my God! It's NOT Terrence!! ANDY nearly soils himself, diving down to fumble with the transformer, suddenly all thumbs. He switches the power on again.

THE NURSE STATION

The fat, sour looking duty NURSE sees the alarm from the failed life support system. She's about to call for help when the indicator stops flashing. She watches it intently for a few SECONDs, nothing. She decides to dismiss it.

TERRENCE'S ROOM

The old man is lying back down, asleep. He seems to be okay. His support machinery is functioning normally again.

With a sigh of relief, ANDY turns and pulls back the curtain behind him. There's Terrence, sans oxygen tent, hooked up to another extensive support system.

                    ANDY
           So. You moved...

He pulls the curtain closed behind him, and moves in close to his uncle. TERRENCE'S expression looks unmistakably morose.

                    ANDY
You don't look happy... Um, I don't usually go in for this stuff, but..
    (He crosses himself, and says a
             silent prayer)
                    Amen.

ANDY leans down, opens the transformer box, and flips the power switch. The machines power down- all except the EKG monitor, which shows a flat line and emits the familiar steady tone. ANDY switches off the monitor. Silence.

TERRENCE'S body is completely still, peaceful. He leans down over its face and speaks in a soft voice.

                    ANDY
       Uncle Terrence? Can you hear me?

TERRENCE'S body remains motionless.

AT THE NURSE'S STATION

This time the NURSE doesn't wait to respond. Seeing the indicators from TERRENCE'S room, she presses the intercom.

                    NURSE
       Chambre 411. Code bleu! Code bleu!

IN TERRENCE'S ROOM

Silence. ANDY's worried. He takes his uncle by the shoulders.

              ANDY
   Come on... Skip the undead
   orientation and get down here.

Nothing. He looks at the door nervously.

OUTSIDE THE DOOR

SERAFINE sees a squad of doctors and NURSEs pushing trolleys of emergency equipment her way from the far end of the hall. She leans her head in the door to warn ANDY.

INT. HOSPITAL ROOM

ANDY is beside himself with stress. He shakes TERRENCE'S bed a little to rouse him. Nothing. He tries a little harder shake... The door opens. It's SERAFINE, also in a panic.

          SERAFINE
    They're coming!

            ANDY
   Shit. What have I done?
      (to SERAFINE)
Stall them! I'll meet you out back.

She shuts the door, just in time. The emergency team are right there.

          SERAFINE
    (feigning hysterics)
Stay away from him! You butchers! Haven't you done enough already!

They struggle to get past her.

INT. HOSPITAL ROOM

ANDY can hear SERAFINE arguing outside the door. He looks out the window to the three story drop into the alley below.

OUTSIDE THE DOOR

SERAFINE is finally shoved aside. They push the door open.

INSIDE

ANDY rushes to the door and pushes it shut. He cranks the DOORKNOB all the over and bends it down, jamming it in the locked position. He steps away. The door holds, but for how long? He looks at the old man in the oxygen tent. Hmm. He pushes the old ma n's bed up against the door.

ANDY forces the window open and steps out onto the ledge. He looks back at his uncle, and the old guy. He shrugs apologetically, then takes a deep breath, closes his eyes, and jumps.

OUTSIDE THE HOSPITAL ROOM DOOR

The fat NURSE is getting impatient with the doctors, who are attempting to pick the lock "surgically". She pushes them aside and heaves her considerable heft against into the door. It opens a crack. She backs up and slams it again....

INSIDE THE ROOM

The NURSE's jolts shake the old guy's bed, sliding it forward. He dozes happily like a baby rocking in the cradle.

EXT. THE BACK ALLEY BEHIND THE HOSPITAL

ANDY runs behind a nearby dumpster to avoid being seen from the window above. He kicks the wall in frustration.

                ANDY
            Damn it!!

A voice calls out from behind ANDY.

           TERRENCE'S voice
Whoa! What an outrageous nightmare!

ANDY spins around and sees Terrence, the undead version, perched atop some trash bags, scratching himself.

                ANDY
          Uncle Terrence?

                TERRENCE
          ANDY? ANDY is that you?

                  ANDY
         Yeah. Look, uncle Terrence-

Terrence mutters distractedly, excitedly, and quickly...

                TERRENCE
    ANDY, I have to tell you about the
       dream I had- or that I'm still
     having - it feels like a systemic,
        physio-tropic reaction to some
          drug, maybe a tryptamine or
      phenethylamine derivative. But it
       is hyper-real. I'd swear my legs
         had been cut off or... wait a
         SECOND... I'm getting a strange
      meta-physical buzz. Shit. I'm, uh,
                dead, aren't I?

                   ANDY
                 Sort of...

BACK IN THE HOSPITAL ROOM

The doctors have clustered around TERRENCE'S corpse. The NURSE is lubricating the electro-shock paddles for the doctor. SERAFINE slips out the door into the hallway.

SOMEONE'S POV, spying from behind a supply cart in the hallway (we see a hand on the cart), watches SERAFINE walk away, unnoticed by the doctors.

BACK IN THE ALLEY

              TERRENCE
Undead. Right. Sort of an ecto-cosmic manifestation. What a pisser. Tell you one thing though, Timothy Leary will be jealous as hell.

                    ANDY
    Great, but listen, I need to know
          where you hid the ADM?

                  TERRENCE
    The ADM! Be careful, ANDY. It's
    very powerful. How do you know
                 about it?

                    ANDY
    I went to St. Severin church.
      (Terrence reacts "I see...")
               Now look-

IN TERRENCE'S ROOM

ZAP! The doctor jolts TERRENCE'S chest with the paddles.

IN THE ALLEY

TERRENCE'S zombie jerks with sudden pain.

                    TERRENCE
       Oh shit! No! ANDY, don't let them
                 take me back there!

                     ANDY
        The ADM! Quickly! Where is it?!

TERRENCE'S ROOM

ZZT! They zap him again.

IN THE BACK ALLEY

                     ANDY
             Where is it! Please!

                    TERRENCE
          AHHH!! The wine cellar!! In a
       bottle of Chateau Margaux. A metal
       cylinder... Don't... Don't- AAAAH!

Another zap. The undead Terrence twists his face in pain. In the background, SERAFINE appears at the mouth of the alley. Terrence croaks out a few last words.

                    TERRENCE
          Lies! All lies! Ahhhh!!!

ANDY turns towards SERAFINE, then back to his uncle, but Terrence is gone.

INT. HOSPITAL ROOM

TERRENCE'S face is contorted with pain. The EKG monitor shows a weak but regular heartbeat. The doctor pulls off his mask and wipes his brow. The other TECHNICIANs congratulate him.

IN THE ALLEY

SERAFINE approaches. ANDY runs up to join her.

ANDY

I saw him. Just before those bastards zapped him back. The ADM is in the wine cellar, in a bottle of Chateau Margaux.

SERAFINE

I didn't know he had a wine cellar.

ANDY

Guess that's why he hid it there. Let's go.

They run out of the alley and see GASTON jump on his hopped-up Kawasaki enduro.

SERAFINE

Oh shit! He must have heard us.

GASTON sees them, gives them the finger and tears off down the street.

                    ANDY
            Dammit! C'mon!

They run to SERAFINE's Vespa- the tires are slashed. Enraged, she kicks it over.

                  SERAFINE
            That bastard! Fuck!

ANDY looks around desperately. A GUY pulls his motorcycle out of its parking spot and starts up the street towards ANDY. ANDY jumps out in front of the accelerating bike and grabs the handlebars, stopping it short, sending the rider tumbling forward, over ANDY. He lands on his butt in the street and starts yelling at ANDY, who climbs on the bike.

                    ANDY
            Sorry... I'll bring it back.

SERAFINE hops on the back and they burn rubber down the street after GASTON. Music cue: CCR's "Bad Moon on the Rise". They screech around the corner onto

SAINT GERMAIN BOULEVARD

It's red lights as far as the eye can see. ANDY grits his teeth and accelerates towards the cluster of traffic stopped at the FIRST light.

                SERAFINE
                Oh merde!

She shuts her eyes as ANDY zooms between the rows of stopped cars and roars through the red light. SCREECH!! Crossing cars slam on their brakes and swerve to avoid the speeding bike. ANDY bears down on the next red light.

                    SERAFINE

               Are you crazy!?

                     ANDY

          Before Hemingway, there was Starsky
                   and Hutch.

ANDY speeds through more stopped cars and runs the next red light. SCREECH!! More swerving cars. ANDY has to swerve himself to avoid one. He bears down on the next light. Meanwhile...

GASTON

is stopped on his bike, casually talking on a cellular phone, two red lights ahead of ANDY and SERAFINE. He hears their bike and turns to see them zoom through the intersection in back of him. GASTON curses, puts the phone in his pocket and twists his throttle, accelerating through the red light.

ANDY AND SERAFINE

gain on GASTON. They're seventy-five yards behind him.

GASTON

pulls a pistol and aims over his shoulder. BANG! He fires back at them.

SERAFINE

pulls her pistol out. Both bikes roar through another red light.

A POLICE CAR pulls out onto the boulevard and turns on its flashing lights and siren and pursues the bikes. The traffic lights turn green.

GASTON leads by fifty yards. The COP car pulls alongside ANDY and

SERAFINE. She discreetly pockets her gun. The COP in the passenger seat aims his gun at ANDY.

                    COP
                  (French)
              Pull over! Now!

                    ANDY
                    Shit!

There's no choice. They pull over. GASTON speeds safely away, looking back at them and laughing. The COP car stops ahead of them and the COPS get out, guns drawn.

                 FIRST COP
                  (French)
           Hands in the air! Now!

ANDY and SERAFINE put up their hands. The FIRST COP goes back to check the police radio, which is beeping. The SECOND COP keeps his gun aimed at ANDY's head. He's furious.

SECOND COP
(French)
Hot shot huh? You know how many officers die in high speed chases?

SERAFINE
(French)
Moron! The guy ahead of us has a gun! He's the one you should stop!

SECOND COP
Shut up! I don't need you to tell me my job. It's always "the other guy"!

SERAFINE
He's going to kill people you ignorant shithead!

                    SECOND COP
             Okay! That's it! You're under
             arrest! Maybe you'll learn some
                    respect in jail!

SERAFINE curses again. ANDY tries to calm her down. The arguing escalates... In the car, the FIRST COP is talking on the radio.

                    FIRST COP
                      Really?

He turns, looks out his window and sees

RENE AND FRANCOIS

parked in their unmarked car. RENE is talking with him on the radio. FRANCOIS waves.

THE SECOND COP

is trying to put handcuffs on SERAFINE. She's still screaming at him. He's incensed. The FIRST COP gets out of the car and walks up to them.

>   FIRST COP
>   (to ANDY and SERAFINE)
>   You can go.

His PARTNER looks at him, incredulous, red-faced.

>   SECOND COP
>   (French- to FIRST COP)
>   WHAT!?

>   FIRST COP
>   (ignores 2nd COP)
>   Drive safely.

>   ANDY
>   Merci.

SERAFINE smiles at the SECOND COP. ANDY peels out, races through the red light and disappears down the boulevard. The COPs watch them go, then turn to each other. The SECOND COP is apoplectic- about to explode.

INT. UNMARKED CAR

RENE and FRANCOIS speed off to keep pace with ANDY. RENE is dialling his cellular phone. As they pass the other police car, we glimpse the two COPs in an angry shoving match against the car. RENE's call goes through.

INT. SAINT SEVERIN CHURCH

LEDUC is on the balcony, studying the stained glass panels and consulting an old book. The cellular phone in his coat pocket rings. An OLD PRIEST nearby frowns at him.

                    LEDUC
             (French- into phone)
                    Hello.
                   (Pause)
I'll meet you there in ten minutes.

He hangs up. The priest is still frowning at him. LEDUC shrugs gruffly- "what do you want from me?" and turns back to the stained glass.

As the church bells sound ten o'clock we cut to different panels: Several scenes of werewolves terrorizing people. A scene where some people mix potions and dump a strange flower into a cauldron. Another shows an evil looking man shaking his arm defiantly at a frowning sun- though he is human his raised arm is the enlarged, hairy limb of a werewolf. Another shows a saint throwing the strange flower into a fire in the town square.

> LEDUC
> (French)
> Thank God for Saint Severin.

The bells strike ten. LEDUC checks his watch, closes his book and hurries off.

EXT. TERRENCE'S APT. BUILDING

Music cue: "Evil" by Howlin' Wolf. GASTON stops, jumps off his bike, and runs into the court yard.

ANDY AND SERAFINE

speed along on the bike, weaving through narrow side streets.

GASTON

riding the wire cage elevator in the apartment building down to the basement. He gets out and walks down the dank hallway, past several padlocked doors. He stops at one with a MCDERMOTT nameplate. He's about to shoot it off, then looking around, thinks again. He grabs the lock and, grimacing with the effort, twists it off with his bare hands.

ANDY AND SERAFINE

stuck behind a garbage truck on a narrow street. ANDY hops the curb and races down the sidewalk, scattering pedestrians.

GASTON

flicks on the light switch in the wine cellar. There are six large racks of wine bottles. He walks past them, scanning the bottles. He stops at the third rack and removes a bottle. The label reads "Chateau Margaux". He tries to peer inside, but it's too hard to see. Instead, he hurls it at the wall- SMASH!! Wine sprays everywhere, but no metal cylinder. He grabs another bottle. SMASH!! Just wine. He grabs another...

ANDY AND SERAFINE

arrive in front of the apartment and hop off their bike. SERAFINE eyes GASTON'S BIKE hatefully. ANDY pulls her along.

            SERAFINE
        Wait a SECOND...

She pulls out her gun. BLAM! BLAM! She blasts the gas tank- WOOF! The bike goes up in a fireball. SERAFINE nods, satisfied. ANDY looks at her like she's nuts. They rush into the courtyard.

GASTON

throws another bottle. SMASH! Just wine. The floor is awash in the pricey Burgundy. He throws another bottle. SMASH! Nothing. He licks his fingers. He's enjoying this...

SERAFINE AND ANDY

In the elevator, going down, maddeningly slowly. Through the window they can see the full moon in the sky. ANDY checks his watch. They look at each other nervously.

GASTON

Throws another- SMASH! A small METAL CYLINDER clinks as it bounces on the floor. GASTON picks it up and smiles. BANG! A gunshot hits GASTON in the arm- he drops the cylinder. SERAFINE and ANDY stand in the doorway.

           SERAFINE
       Dirty bastard...

SERAFINE fires again- BANG! The shot misses as GASTON hits the deck and draws his gun in one very fast motion, taking aim at ANDY who's rushing towards him.

           GASTON
     That's far enough!

ANDY stops, GASTON's gun aimed at his chest. SERAFINE steps slowly towards GASTON, her gun aimed at him.

                    GASTON
                (to SERAFINE)
        Another step and he's dead!

                    ANDY
        Go ahead SERAFINE. Blow him away.

SERAFINE stops. The three of them stand there in a close triangle, the metal cylinder on the floor between them. It's a Mexican standoff... in Paris. Then...

                    CLAUDE (O.S.)
            Drop the gun!

CLAUDE is in the doorway holding a pistol. SERAFINE sees him and turns back to GASTON, smiling.

> SERAFINE
> (to GASTON)
> You heard him. Do it!

GASTON just smiles back at her. CLAUDE steps forwards and cocks his gun against SERAFINE's head.

> CLAUDE
> I said drop the gun.

SERAFINE's expression turns confused, horrified. ANDY is shocked. She drops the gun. CLAUDE picks it up and pockets it, keeping his gun on SERAFINE, who stares at him, aghast.

> ANDY
> You bastard! God! I should've known. You wanted the cure all for yourself!

> GASTON
> Cure!? Ha-ha-ha!

ANDY and SERAFINE react with confusion to GASTON's outburst. CLAUDE picks up the metal cylinder and unscrews its cap with his free hand. He slides out a vial filled with amber fluid and holds it to up to the light. He smiles.

                  CLAUDE
No, it's no cure. It's something much more interesting.

                 SERAFINE
You fucking liar!

                  CLAUDE
           (with mock alarm)
Oh, did I hurt the little GIRL's feelings? Well excusez moi...
           (CONTINUED...)

           CLAUDE (Cont'd)
I confess my desire for ADM is quite "intense". So I deceived you

and our poor friend Terry- a competent TECHNICIAN, but let's face it, a bit naive. "The great cure for lycanthropy!" Hmph. He didn't have the vision to grasp the potential of ADAM, until it was too late. And even then, he came rushing down to tell <u>me</u>, as if I would be just as shocked! Ha.

He pockets the vial, pulls out the white "cyanide" tablet and pops it in his mouth. ANDY reacts with shock.

                CLAUDE
    (off ANDY's look, crunching up
         tablet in his mouth)
Oh this? Rolaids. I had a midnight snack that... disagreed with me. SERAFINE's been doing a slow burn. She explodes and lunges at CLAUDE, knocking his gun out of his hand.

                    SERAFINE

                Fucking traitor!

She picks CLAUDE up and **hurls him across the room.** CRASH!! CLAUDE smashes into a rack of wine bottles. SERAFINE jumps after him and dives on top of him pummelling him in a blind rage. ANDY looks at her, agog.

                      ANDY

                Wait a SECOND...

He and GASTON notice CLAUDE's gun at the same time. They both dive for it. ANDY grabs it but GASTON steps on his hand and aims his gun down at him.

                     GASTON

                You want to be cured?

He cocks the gun. ANDY lets go of CLAUDE's gun. GASTON picks it up and aims one gun at ANDY and the other at SERAFINE, who's wrestling with CLAUDE. CLAUDE throws her off and she lands on her butt next to ANDY. ANDY looks at SERAFINE.

                ANDY
    What the fuck!? You too!?

             SERAFINE
         (stammering)
  I... I didn't think you would... I'm sorry... I believed that son-of-a-bitch...

CLAUDE gets to his feet, drenched with wine and smarting from SERAFINE's punches. He walks over to SERAFINE and kicks her in the face.

CLAUDE

Shut up, you foul mouthed little cunt. I don't have time for your histrionics.

GASTON

Give me the ADM old man.

GASTON is aiming one of his guns at CLAUDE.

CLAUDE

Oh for Christ's sakes GASTON. Can't you rise above the level of common thug just this once?

GASTON

Give it to me!

CLAUDE

Don't be an idiot. There are certain procedures one must-

GASTON

NOW!

CLAUDE sighs. He takes the vial from his pocket and walks over to GASTON.

CLAUDE
Very well then...

GASTON grabs the vial, uncaps it and drinks it down greedily. He stands there, waiting. Nothing happens...

ANDY
Ha. Some wonder drug...

GASTON
Why isn't it doing anything!?

CLAUDE
I told you. It's not ready.

CLAUDE turns to the noise of footsteps and a walkie-talkie in the hallway. Four uniformed officers plus RENE and FRANCOIS storm into the room, guns drawn.

                    COPS
              (French/English)
        Freeze! Drop your weapons! Hands
                     up!

ANDY and SERAFINE put up their hands. GASTON brandishes his guns at the COPs, then sees the six guns aimed at him and drops it. LEDUC walks in.

                   CLAUDE
              (French- to LEDUC)
        Thank God! These hoodlums tried to
                    rob me!
                   LEDUC
              (French- to CLAUDE)
              Put up your hands.

                   CLAUDE
                   (French)
                  But surely-

LEDUC cocks his pistol and aims it at CLAUDE.

> LEDUC
> (French)
> Now!

CLAUDE puts his hands up.

> CLAUDE
> (French)
> What's the charge?

> LEDUC
> (French)
> There is no charge.
> (English)
> Everybody comes in for a few questions. Everything checks out, you will go free. <u>After</u> midnight.

CLAUDE frowns. GASTON swears. ANDY looks at SERAFINE, shocked and confused. She looks back at him, angry and sad.

cut to:

EXT. STREET - NIGHT

The COPs are herding the handcuffed "questionees" into the back of a reinforced paddy wagon. LEDUC talks to the DRIVER, and another COP in the passenger seat.

                    LEDUC
                  (French)
      Godard is waiting for you at
      Rocherout jail. Hurry... And don't
         stop for anything. Good luck.

The driver nods. It roars off, lights flashing and siren wailing. LEDUC and the other COPs head for their respective cars. LEDUC barks orders to an AID who's at the ready with the car radio.

                    LEDUC
     I want four separate maximum
     security cells ready. Get video
       cameras, photographers, and
                   doctors.

The aid nods and gets on the radio.
LEDUC checks his watch. It's 10:47.

cut to:

INT. PADDY WAGON

SERAFINE hangs her head sullenly, in a quiet rage. She won't meet ANDY's gaze. He looks over at CLAUDE and GASTON. GASTON is restless, edgy. He grabs CLAUDE by the collar and shakes him.

                    GASTON
          Nothing's happening!

                    ANDY
       Looks like he lied to you too.

CLAUDE breaks GASTON's grip and shoves him back in his seat.

                    CLAUDE
                   (calmly)
         Relax my friend. It's still not
                     ready.

ANDY looks back at SERAFINE. He shakes his head in disbelief.

                     ANDY
         Now I remember why I didn't want to
         come to Paris. Everyone you meet is
                 a goddam <u>werewolf</u>!

SERAFINE stares bitterly at her feet.

                   SERAFINE
          I hope they fucking fry us all.

                     ANDY
            Yeah. French fries...

SLAM! He's interrupted by the sound of GASTON's head snapping back against the wall. His eyes bulge wide. He grins and starts to laugh. FIRST a little. Then a lot.

                  GASTON
     Yes! Yes! Ha! Haha hahaha..

He stands up, laughing, power-mad. Suddenly his body is jerked by a spasm and he falls to the floor. He's not laughing anymore. He flails about wildly, croaking out strangled cries, gripped with a terrible seizure.

IN THE FRONT CAB

The TWO GUARDS, the driver and his PARTNER, hear the commotion. The guard looks over to his PARTNER, and chuckles.

                    PARTNER
          Aaooooo!!! Heh heh heh.

They both laugh. The driver takes a
sharp turn at high speed.

IN THE BACK COMPARTMENT

GASTON flops around on the floor
like a fish, grabbed by a flurry of
convulsions. He bites off his
tongue, spitting blood everywhere.
Finally, he goes rigid with one
last seizure, then falls totally
limp. ANDY studies the very dead
corpse.

                     ANDY
        It killed him... You coulda just
            used Draino. It's cheaper.

                    CLAUDE
         I told him it wasn't ready...

CLAUDE takes a folded PAPER CUP from his jacket pocket. He blows into the cup to bring it back into shape. He then takes a SHARPENED STEEL TUBE from his pocket, plunges it into GASTON's neck, and fills the cup with the blood that pours forth. ANDY and SERAFINE are horrified. CLAUDE puts the cup of blood to his lips and pauses.

                    CLAUDE
          <u>Now</u> it's ready.

He swallows the cup of blood down in one gulp, and sits back to wait for the effects, smiling dreamily.

                    CLAUDE
What is the curse of the werewolf? I'll tell you. The <u>curse</u> is to possess such awesome power and yet be completely unconscious of it. It may as well belong to someone else. But it wasn't always that way. A

thousand years ago the Gaul's had a drug powerful enough to unlock the door to lycanthropic consciousness, to full control. It came from moons breath.
(CONTINUED...)

              ANDY (cont'd)
A small white flower once found in the hills of this region, until the thick headed crusade by our famous Saint Severin eradicated it for all eternity. But now, thanks to ADAM, the "curse" is over...

As he says this, he holds up his RIGHT ARM. It begins to mutate and grow, reshaping his arm into the grotesque, powerful forelimb of the beast. PLINK! His swelling wrist pops the handcuff easily.

              SERAFINE
              (French)
        Holy mother of God...

                    ANDY

                 Fuck me...

CLAUDE rises to his feet,
triumphant. He advances towards
ANDY and SERAFINE, backing them up
against the rear doors of the van.
He gently traces the outline of
SERAFINE's face with his werewolf
hand. She bristles at his touch.

                    CLAUDE
    All my life I've worked to unlock
    the power of the unconscious mind.
    Well this is it. <u>This</u> is power!

                    ANDY
     You sure it's not just 'coz you
           jerk off too much?

CLAUDE cocks his werewolf fist and
SLAMS it into the back doors,
inches from ANDY's head. He leaves
a deep dent, and opens the doors

just a crack. It's a gesture that seems calculated to frighten them. It works.

CLAUDE holds up his LEFT ARM and transforms it to match his right. It takes some effort and a little pain, but he keeps a smile on his face throughout the process.

> CLAUDE
> Don't you see what this means? I've broken through! I'm in total control! Not the moon! I can do whatever the fuck I want!

SMASH!! CLAUDE drives his left arm into the back doors, making another huge dent, and opening the crack even wider.

IN THE FRONT CAB

The COPs exchange worried looks. The one on the passenger side slides open the viewing panel. CLAUDE has his back to him.

                    COP
                  (French)
          Hey! What's going on in--

He stops short as CLAUDE turns around, revealing his monstrous arms. Mortified, the COP reaches for the SHOT GUN under the dash. CLAUDE races up towards the view window. As the guard pokes the muzzle through the window, CLAUDE grabs hold of it. BLAM! The guard's shot hits the side wall. CLAUDE rips the gun from the guard angrily, and smashes it to pieces against the wall, grinning like the devil himself.

Meanwhile ANDY throws himself at the doors, kicking them, trying in vain to break them open. He spots the SHOTGUN BARREL on the floor and grabs it.

CLAUDE reaches through the window and grabs the guard by the head. He repeatedly smashes the guard's head against the back wall of the cab.

> CLAUDE
> (as he smashes the guard)
> Don't you know... the wolf... is a protected... species!?

The driver freaks out, seeing his PARTNER get his head crushed. THE PADDY WAGON swerves all over the road.

ANDY uses the shotgun barrel to twist open the lock on the van doors. As the vehicle swerves, he drops the barrel out the door, and falls over. He calls to SERAFINE.

                    ANDY
          I need your help. Come on.

She joins him and together they take a run at the back doors. The doors open a little, but the lock still holds.

Finished with the guard, CLAUDE turns and sees what ANDY and SERAFINE are up to.

                    CLAUDE
                    Wait!

ANDY and SERAFINE take another run- it works. THE DOORS bust open, and ANDY and SERAFINE, still handcuffed, go tumbling out into THE STREET, rolling on the pavement.

SCREECH! HONK! Cars swerve to avoid them, just barely. CRASH! A minivan plows into a parked car. CLAUDE watches from the back of the van. He rears his head to the moon and smiles.

IN THE CAB of the paddy wagon, the driver hears an unearthly howl. It's hellish. Without looking away from the road, he points his pistol through the hole in the compartment. He adjusts THE MIRROR to see into the rear compartment - The back doors are hanging open. He steals a look over his shoulder- Other than GASTON's corpse, it's empty... He breathes a sigh of relief and turns back to the road as-

A HUGE WEREWOLF - CLAUDE fully transformed - bursts through the windshield and rips into him.

THE PADDY WAGON is traveling over the Pont Neuf bridge. A GASOLINE TRUCK approaches from the other direction. The werewolf leaps off of the hood just as the paddy wagon, swerving all over the road, hits the gasoline truck head on.

KA-BOOM!! Both vehicles explode in a fireball, smash through the side wall of the bridge, and plunge into THE RIVER.

INT. SQUAD CAR

LEDUC, following at a distance, is trying in vain to get the paddy wagon driver on the radio.

              LEDUC
  Allo! Jean-Louis! Respond! Allo!

His PARTNER slows the car. Traffic ahead is snarled. It's chaos. He taps LEDUC on the arm and points...

              PARTNER
           Inspector...

LEDUC sees the column of black smoke in the distance.

              LEDUC
   Merde... merde, merde, merde.

He slams his fist against the dash angrily.

CUT TO:

EXT. PARIS STREET, NIGHT

ANDY lies by the roadside, dazed, bruised, handcuffed, but conscious. He sits up unsteadily, and looks for SERAFINE.

ANDY

SERAFINE?

He sees a small crowd of people a little further up the road, outside a small bistro. He staggers up to them and pushes his way through. SERAFINE is there on the ground by the curb, eyes closed.

Kneeling beside her, he turns angrily on the onlookers.

ANDY

Get out of here! Go on! Move it!

He shoos them away. Of course, they just back up a bit, still gawking at the handcuffed couple.

ANDY

SERAFINE... Get up, come on...

ANDY brushes away the hair from SERAFINE's face. He feels her neck for a pulse - she has one. But as he takes his hand away, he notices a smudge of BASE MAKE-UP has rubbed off on his fingers. He looks at the back of SERAFINE's neck and sees that the makeup had been covering A SCAR. It bears the unmistakable star shape of the wound ANDY inflicted on the werewolf that bit him.

Horrified, he stands and backs away a few feet. SERAFINE opens her eyes, sees him.

                SERAFINE
               (groggy)
   ANDY?... What? What is it?
 (she sits up, her head clearing)
      ANDY... are you okay?

                          ANDY
         It was you... That night in the
         tunnels. You. You did this to me.

                        SERAFINE
         No I.... ANDY, you can't be sure.

                          ANDY
          That's the scar where I stabbed
          you! Oh God... You deliberately
         took me down there so you could...
              God, I can't believe it!

SERAFINE gets to her feet, a little
unsteadily at FIRST.

                        SERAFINE
          You made me go there. I tried to
            stop you! You wouldn't listen!

                          ANDY
          What was I? Your idea of a fuckin'
                hors d'oeuvre? Huh?

                    SERAFINE
Shut up! You fucking shut up! What
do you want? Huh? What the hell do
                   you want?

She walks over, grabs a steak knife
from one of the outside tables at
the bistro, and charges at ANDY,
pulling open her shirt... She
offers him the knife, and pounds at
her heart.

                    SERAFINE
   Here! Come on! Do it! Go ahead.

                      ANDY
                     What...?

                    SERAFINE
  You know what. Kill me. Cut out my
     fucking heart. Go on! Do it!

Enraged, ANDY takes the knife. He
and SERAFINE lock eyes. For a

SECOND he's tempted, his blood boiling, heart pounding.

              ANDY
        You're crazy.

He throws the knife aside, turns and walks away.

              ANDY
      This is all crazy!

SERAFINE retrieves the knife and chases after him. She gets in front of him and blocks his path. She holds the knife point to her own chest.

            SERAFINE
  The drug was a lie, but the legend in the church is true. Ask the undead.

ANDY just stares back at her, not knowing what to say. It's all too much to believe. He shakes his head. He tries to go, but she moves in front of him. She's determined.

              SERAFINE
     We don't both have to die.

               ANDY
            (softening)
     I couldn't do it. Not to you.

He sees her looking up. He follows her gaze to the FULL MOON. It's getting late. ANDY shudders, wipes the sweat from his brow. He's already starting to feel the heat in his blood.
SERAFINE
I can't go through another night. I won't.

ANDY takes her hand and guides the knife away from her chest.

                         ANDY
        I know... I'm already burning up..
        Look, I'm not going to go through
        this another night either. But we
        still have some time to get CLAUDE.
        He'll just kill more people, and
                   spread the curse.

She's desperate, tears welling up
in her eyes.

                       SERAFINE
          We can't stop him. Not now.
          Handcuffed, with no kind of
            weapons. Please ANDY...

                         ANDY
        No. We have to try. We'll figure
        something out. And if midnight
        comes before we can get to him,
        well, then we go together. Deal?
              (he extends a cuffed hand)
                   Shake a paw?

She laughs despite her tears, puts her cuffed hands over his head and hugs him tightly.

> SERAFINE
> I know where he'll go.

> ANDY
> Where?

> SERAFINE
> Somewhere where there are no police, and plenty to eat.

ANDY looks at her. He knows what she's driving at.

cut to:

EXT. PETIT PONT - NIGHT

LEDUC and NAPIER stand on the bridge, which has been blocked off, watching the tow truck drag the charred wreck of the paddy wagon from the river. Ambulances wait nearby. Firemen are still putting out small piles of flaming debris.

> NAPIER
> (French)
> Poor Bazin and Racine. At least they brought those monsters down with them.

LEDUC isn't listening- he sees something that makes his face go slack: The paddy wagon emerges from the murky water revealing the open, banged-up back door with several large FIST PRINTS in it. He checks his watch- it's 11:32.

> LEDUC
> (French- to himself)
> Impossible...
> (to NAPIER- urgent)
> Get headquarters on the radio.

NAPIER isn't paid to ask questions. He hops to it.

                NAPIER
        Right away sir.

cut to:

INT. UNDERGROUND PARTY - NIGHT

ANDY and SERAFINE emerge from the tunnel, wearing grim, determined expressions. The party is in full swing- throbbing beats and sweaty dancing bodies. They walk straight across the dance floor, pushing their way through the crowd. Amongst the variety o f freaky types here, no one raises an eyebrow at two people in handcuffs.

SERAFINE, who's scanning the room, is approached by a leather clad HIPSTER GUY.

                    HIPSTER GUY
            SERAFINE, mon belle! Ca va?

He goes to kiss her on both cheeks.
Without breaking stride, she puts
her handcuffed hands on his face
and shoves, sending him reeling.

SERAFINE points out a gang of four
militant SKINHEADs off in a corner.
ANDY nods and smiles.

                      ANDY
              This could be fun.

They make their way to the
SKINHEADs. ANDY walks up to the
SKINHEAD LEADER, who's got a
swastika tattoo, a bad disposition,
and a fifty-pound advantage on
ANDY.

                      ANDY
          I got something you want. Follow
                       me.

ANDY and SERAFINE walk into A SMALL CHAMBER off the main space. The SKINHEAD signals his mates to come along, slips on some BRASS KNUCKLES, and follows ANDY into

THE CHAMBER

The SKINHEADs surround ANDY and SERAFINE. There's no one else in the room. The SKINHEAD leader looks at ANDY's handcuffs and sniggers.

              SKINHEAD
    What do you got, pervert?

                ANDY
  I got Hitler's dick in a jar. And the funny thing is it's still in Goerring's mouth.

The SKINHEAD turns red with rage and throws a punch at ANDY's head.

With lightning speed, ANDY grabs the SKINHEAD's fist, twists his arm around his back and hurls him across the room. He slams face FIRST into the stone wall and collapses on the floor with a THUD.

Simultaneously, the other three SKINHEADs attack. SERAFINE BASHES one across the face with both fists, sending him to the floor. The other gets her in a headlock from behind. She runs backwards and- SLAM!- crushes him against the wall.

The third SKINHEAD tries to kick ANDY in the groin. ANDY grabs his boot and flips him over backwards- he actually does a full back flip and lands on his face.

The leader groggily pulls a pistol and aims it at ANDY. ANDY snatches it out of his hand.

                    ANDY
           Didn't even have to ask.

                  SERAFINE
                  (French)
        All your weapons, on the floor!
                    Now!

The SKINHEADs slide out some LEAD PIPES, a SWITCHBLADE, another PISTOL, and an army surplus GRENADE. ANDY and SERAFINE scoop them up, except the lead pipes.

                    ANDY
           Neo-Nazis. Ya gotta love 'em.
                (to the SKINHEADs)
           Merci beau coup, monsieurs.

cut to:

INT. TUNNEL - NIGHT

Music cue: "After Midnight (we're gonna let it all hang out)". ANDY's gun is pressed against the chain on SERAFINE's handcuffs- BANG! The chain is broken. BANG! She returns the favour and his chain is broken.

They walk into the DRIPPING, dank tunnel, away from the party, which fades away in the background. Each carries a pistol and a flashlight. BEADS OF SWEAT appear on their foreheads.

The tunnel tilts downhill. Heavier DRIPPING. They turn a corner and...

SLAM! Something barrels into them- it's a HYSTERICAL GIRL. She's about nineteen and splattered with blood. She SCREAMS uncontrollably. SERAFINE holds her by the shoulders, trying to calm her.

                    GIRL
                  (French)
    Ahhhhhhhh! A monster! My God! It
      got my boyfriend! Nooooo!

                  SERAFINE
          Ou!? Ou est le monstre!?

                    GIRL
    Ahhhh! Let me go! Let me gooooo!!

She's off the deep end, flailing at SERAFINE, who keeps trying to calm her down. There's no time for this. ANDY presses his gun to her temple. She shuts up and stares at him with wide, terror stricken eyes.

                    ANDY
                (calm, firm)
            Ou est le monstre?

She points back down the tunnel she came out of.

                    GIRL
                  (French)
              Down the stairs.

                    ANDY
                   Merci.

He lets her go. She starts SCREAMING again and continues on, disappearing into darkness. ANDY winces and holds his ears.

                  SERAFINE
            No wonder he let her go.

                    ANDY
                   Really.

They run in the direction she pointed. They arrive at the intersection with A STAIRWAY to the right. They start down it. They see something up ahead- SOMEONE'S HAND is sticking out on the ground from a passage at a landing on the staircase.

                    SERAFINE
               Her boyfriend.

The hand moves a bit, pulls back and disappears into the crossing passage.

                    ANDY
               He's alive. C'mon.

They hurry down to the landing, shine their light into the passage. The hand is severed, and A BIG RAT is dragging it along with some difficulty. A dozen or other rats munch on scraps of flesh scattered over a grisly mess of blood and body parts. ANDY and SERAFINE stare at it for a moment. Suddenly ANDY looks away.

                    ANDY
           God. I can't believe it.

                   SERAFINE
                    What?

                    ANDY
                  (disturbed)
             It's making me hungry.

A beast HOWL echoes through the tunnels. SERAFINE shines he flashlight on some bloody beast foot/paw prints leading down the stairs.

They follow the bloody prints down the stairs and come to an ancient ARCHED DOORWAY with a skull set in the arch and a chiselled inscription. ANDY points to the inscription.

                    ANDY
              What does it say?

                    SERAFINE
                    (reading)
"Stop! Beyond this passage lie the catacombs of Paris: the exclusive domain of the dead."

ANDY gestures back to the bloody remains.

                    ANDY
         We'll say we're with him.

They walk through the gate and enter

THE CATACOMBS

ANDY shines his flashlight around, illuminating two large tunnels which lead into a twisting, intestinal maze, lined from floor to ceiling with HUMAN SKULLS and FEMURS. The bones form the building blocks of the tunnel walls and are arranged in various patterns- from crucifixes to Masonic pyramids and even pentagrams. Ground water seeps from the ceilings and walls, DRIPPING over the eroded, crumbling bones.

Despite the situation, ANDY can't help but be dumb struck by the spectacular necropolis.

              ANDY
              Whoa...

            SERAFINE
   After the revolution, the Paris cemeteries overflowed. They dug up all the old bodies and brought them here. Seven million people. Mostly very poor.

            ANDY
   Pretty stylish digs for a bunch of paupers.

SERAFINE

Well, they <u>are</u> French.

ANDY

Right.

Another eerie HOWL echoes through the maze. ANDY looks down both main tunnels- the howl seems to come from each of them.

ANDY

These tunnels must loop around and connect.

SERAFINE

Let's go from both ends. We'll cut him off.

ANDY considers this.

ANDY

Okay. Be careful.

                    SERAFINE
                    You too.

She kisses him. They're both sweating heavily now. She starts off to the right. He watches her go for a moment and then walks down the other skull lined tunnel.
cut to:

EXT. PETIT PONT - NIGHT

The CHARRED BODIES of GASTON and the two COPs lie on the river bank, near the wreck. LEDUC surveys them with a few other COPs. NAPIER leans out of a nearby car with a radio handset. The bells of nearby Notre Dame begin to ring.

                    NAPIER
                   (French)
        It's headquarters sir. They got a
                    report.

LEDUC rushes over and grabs the handset.

                    LEDUC
              (French- into radio)
              What've you got?

              DESK OFFICER (V.O.)
         Just a crazy call from a GIRL,
         probably fucked up on drugs. I
         wouldn't bother you but you said
              call with <u>anything</u> unusual.

                    LEDUC
              What did she say?

              DESK OFFICER (V.O.)
           Something about a monster,
         underground, in the catacombs under
                    Place Denfert.

                    LEDUC
         I need two tactical assault squads
         at Place Denfert immediately. You

>   can tell the commissioner it's a
>   code red.
>
>   DESK OFFICER (V.O.)
>   But Inspector, this GIRL, I
>   wouldn't call her reliable.
>
>   LEDUC
>   Now!
>
>   DESK OFFICER (V.O.)
>   Yes sir.

LEDUC throws the handset back at NAPIER. The church bells strike twelve.

cut to:

INT. CATACOMBS
ANDY walks along carefully, shining the flashlight ahead of him, his gun at the ready. His breathing gets heavier. His face gets redder.

More sweat. His heart pounds in his ears.

The tunnel follows a serpentine path, with many smaller passages and anterooms off to the sides.

ANDY sees some flickering light reflecting off the wet skulls up ahead. He approaches it. It's coming out of AN ANTECHAMBER. He holds his gun out in front of him and steps quietly. He peers into the antechamber and finds

TWO HALF EATEN BODIES

It's the old hag and the wino he saw in the tunnels at the FIRST party. They've been killed very recently- blood still drips from their gaping wounds.

He kneels over the wino's body. There's a big chunk missing from his neck. ANDY stares at the BLOODY FLESH, transfixed. He shudders with a sudden spasm. His breathing gets quicker. More sweat. He reaches towards the wound, his hand shaking, and touches the flesh. Blood runs down his fingers. He slowly brings his hand back towards his mouth.

              TERRENCE (O.S.)
   Don't do it, ANDY. Fight it with
       everything you've got.

ANDY looks up to see UNCLE TERRENCE, stumps and all, sitting across from him.

                  ANDY
      Uncle Terrence, you're...

                TERRENCE
   Yeah, I finally "checked out",
   thank God. But there's a bit of
       unfinished business.

                    ANDY
                   CLAUDE.

                  TERRENCE
        I never thought I'd ask this of
         anyone, ANDY, but do me a favour
         and kill the evil son-of-a-bitch,
                  will you?

A SNARL cuts him off. ANDY jumps
up, steps out into the main tunnel
and shines his light.

THE BEAST

rounds a curve and comes into view
about thirty yards away. It's
running straight at ANDY and
closing fast. ANDY aims the gun.
BANG! A miss- the bullet shatters a
skull on the wall. BANG! Another
miss. BANG! The bullet hits the
beast in the shoulder. I t stumbles

but keeps coming. BANG! A miss. ANDY aims carefully.

                    ANDY
            C'mon you mother...

BANG! A direct hit in the chest. The beast falls. Snarling in pain.

BANG! ANDY blasts again, but the beast drags itself to the safety of a recessed area off the tunnel, out of ANDY's line of fire. ANDY walks forward, listening to the horrible wails of the beast, thrashing around in a puddle on the floor.

ANDY aims his gun and his flashlight as he nears the corner of the recess. The wailing and thrashing settles down. ANDY proceeds cautiously. He rounds the corner, and shines the light on

SERAFINE

naked, bleeding from bullet wounds in the chest, shoulder, and neck. She lies still. ANDY sighs with anguish. He drops to his knees.

                    ANDY
               No! Oh God!

He puts down his gun and cradles her head in his hands. She's breathing- just barely. She looks into his eyes. Her voice is weak.

                    ANDY
             Oh God. Shit...

                  SERAFINE
                  ANDY...

She reaches up feebly and manages to grab the SWITCHBLADE from his back pocket. She clicks it open and hands it to ANDY.

                    SERAFINE
                    Do it.

ANDY's shaking, shuddering- his breathing erratic.

                    ANDY
                    No. It's over.

He shakily presses the gun to his own head.

                    TERRENCE (O.S.)
                    Don't, ANDY. Stop CLAUDE.

ANDY looks up. Terrence, MARCEL, AMY, and a dozen other mutilated, rotting undead, presumably SERAFINE's victims, stand in the tunnel, looking on solemnly.

                    MARCEL (O.S.)
                    Either way works for us…

                    AMY
            But you better hurry.

CLAUDE's stentorian voice echo's
from beyond a curve in the tunnel.

                 CLAUDE (O.S.)
            You can't turn back ANDY.

CLAUDE

in human form, walks towards the
glow from ANDY's flashlight around
the bend. His naked body is taut
and muscular- it looks thirty years
younger than it should. His face is
younger too- he looks the picture
of a powerful young warrior.

CLAUDE
"Man is something to be <u>surpassed</u>!
A rope, stretched over the abyss
between the animal and the
Superman". Nietzsche was right,
ANDY. And now, I have crossed that

abyss. I am no longer man OR beast, but man AND beast. ADAM has lived up to its name. I am the FIRST new man, and my God it is FUCKING MAGNIFICENT! You're already half way there ANDY. Feel the power in your veins. With ADAM, you could harness it. Master it. Let it transform you into something more glorious than your wildest dreams!

ANDY

is shaking violently- on the brink of transforming. SERAFINE raises the blade to him again. She's fading fast.

                   SERAFINE
 Don't let me die for nothing...

ANDY winces with pain- his brow bulges, his teeth enlarge, the transformation is starting. Uncle Terrence is worried.

                    TERRENCE
                     ANDY!

CLAUDE

still walking. The light is getting
brighter- he's almost around the
bend. He's buzzing with a scary
kind of euphoria.

                    CLAUDE
The choice is yours ANDY: deny your
    own blood, die an unfulfilled
  child, or face the challenge of
mind and body united at last. Which
               will it be?

He rounds the corner and sees ANDY
hunched over SERAFINE's body. He
keeps walking.

               CLAUDE (cont'd)
 Don't be confused by old beliefs.
 This is beyond mere words like good
    or evil. You have to <u>feel</u> it!

ANDY

whips around, BLOOD streaming from his mouth, gun aimed, grip rock solid, his features back to normal, eyes locked on the beast with determined, controlled rage.

                    ANDY
               Feel *this*.

BLAM! BLAM! He pumps out two shots. One hits CLAUDE in the upper left part of his CHEST. The other hits his CHEEK, exits at the back of his jaw and shatters the cheekbone of A SKULL on the wall behind him. He screams in pain and dives for cover into a SMALL INTERSECTING TUNNEL.

ANDY gets up, pausing for a SECOND to look back at SERAFINE's face. It looks peaceful. The undead are gone. He starts after CLAUDE.

CLAUDE

sits leaning against a wall of skulls. The face wound is bleeding but not mortal.

>   CLAUDE
>   Stupid boy...

With an awesome rage he grimaces and starts to TRANSFORM HIS LEFT SIDE- his muscles swell around the chest wound and THE BULLET actually squeezes out of the hole and falls to the ground. The wound closes up as the flesh keeps morphing and growing hair.

ANDY

creeps around the corner, gun and flashlight aimed, towards the small tunnel.

When the flashlight beam falls on CLAUDE, he's in mid pounce- rocketing at ANDY with bad intent. BANG! ANDY gets off a shot- it hits CLAUDE in his THIGH as he tackles ANDY.

They wrestle, CLAUDE in mid-transformation, his left side further along, hairier, his facial bones shifting. His thigh swells and ripples and THE BULLET SQUIRTS OUT of its wound.

His left arm, mostly transformed, grips ANDY's gun hand. BANG! ANDY squeezes off a shot, blowing off the tip of CLAUDE's transforming THUMB.

CRUNCH! CLAUDE clamps his vice like grip and crushes the gun. ANDY wrenches his hand away as CLAUDE hurls him off like a rag doll.

ANDY flies through the air and SMASHES into the tunnel wall. The wall of ancient SKULLS and BONES shatters and collapses around ANDY- burying him in ossified fragments.

ANDY lifts himself out of the pile and looks at CLAUDE, who lies on the floor finishing his transformation. His right side is catching up with his left and his head is now more beast than human. All the while he glares at ANDY and doesn't appear vulnerable.

ANDY takes advantage of the moment to get the hell away- he runs into the tunnel, leaving CLAUDE behind to finish transforming.

ANDY makes a few quick turns through the maze- it seems he has evaded CLAUDE for the moment. He pulls the GRENADE from his pocket, turns off his flashlight and pads along softly, listening for the beast.

Suddenly a sharp sound from behind him makes ANDY jump.

              VOICE
        (French- screaming)
  STOP WHERE YOU ARE! HANDS UP!

ANDY turns around. A scared COP is aiming his gun at him, shining a flashlight in his face. ANDY puts his hands up.

              COP
          (English)
  It's you. You should be dead in that wreck with Bazin and Racine!

              ANDY
  Shhh! Be quiet, man! We're not alone-

                    COP

Shut up! Save your stories. The
only thing I want to hear is you
begging for your life. I want to
see you suffer, like they did.
(he sees ANDY's look of terror)
Haha! You're scared now, eh? Come
on. Where's the scary monster now
huh? Ha ha... We'll see who-

A ROAR cuts him off. The COP spins around- the beam from his flashlight flooding THE BEAST with light as it springs through the air at him. ANDY runs.

                    COP
                 (French)
                 My God!

He gets off one shot- it hits the beast in the arm, but it's too late. The beast clamps its massive jaw onto the COP's neck and bites his head clean off. THE HEAD rolls across the floor and comes to rest in a pile of skulls.

cut to:

SERAFINE'S BODY

In the tunnel. Two queasy COPs stand over it. LEDUC approaches them.

              LEDUC
            (French)
     What have you got?

              COP
      (French- disturbed)
 It's the GIRL. Someone cut out her
            heart.

              LEDUC
       (Matter of factly)
             Good.

The COPs look at him like he's nuts.

cut to:

ANDY

is crouched at a corner of two catacomb tunnels, grenade clutched in his hand. He hears something and carefully peers around the corner.

ANDY'S POV

At the end of the long tunnel of bones, the beast lurks at another intersection, sniffing the air and growling, some forty yards away.

ANDY ducks back around the corner. He holds up the grenade, pulls the pin, and whispers a quick prayer...

                         ANDY
                      (to himself)
                  Just throw a strike...

With a determined grunt, he pitches the grenade around the corner and then ducks back. Suddenly the beast's growling stops. ANDY grits his teeth and closes his eyes, awaiting the explosion. Just silence. Then a small skittering sound close by. He opens his eyes.

THE GRENADE

skitters to a stop, a couple of feet from him.

                         ANDY
                         Shit!

He bolts and gets five steps from it when

KA-BOOM!! It explodes behind him, launching him through the air along with a spray of bones and rubble. He lands twenty feet away and clutches his left leg, wincing in pain.

              ANDY
    Ahh! Son of a bitch!

LEDUC

and the COPs turn towards the sound of the blast.

              LEDUC
        (French)
    Let's go.

ANDY

struggles to his feet. He clicks on his flashlight and sees the blast has caved in the tunnel- a wall of rubble seals ANDY off from the beast.

ANDY breathes a sigh of relief. At least he's got time. He starts limping away from the wall of rubble...

SMASH!! The rubble explodes again as the beast crashes through it like a freight train, sending rocks and bones flying.

ANDY runs as fast as he can with his bad leg. The beast closes in on him quickly. ANDY jumps up for a NARROW OPENING in the tunnel ceiling. He grabs the metal rung inside and pulls himself up into the vertical shaft as the beast pounces. The beast catches ANDY's foot with its claw. ANDY pulls out of his sneaker and just barely eludes the beast's grasp.

ANDY climbs up the metal rungs in this old service shaft- barely wide enough for his body. The beast claws and gnashes his teeth at the opening but can't fit in- for now.

ANDY reaches an iron grate, pushes it up and crawls out into

ANOTHER DRIPPY TUNNEL

Like the ones near the party- no skulls. There's a lot of water in this one. It looks familiar.

CLAUDE

is transforming back into human shape. His face is now more human than beast. He screams into the vertical passage in a growling, not quite human voice.

                    CLAUDE
            You have no advantage, ANDY! My
                  body has no limits!

ANDY

looks around in the tunnel. He sees
something (we don't). He limps off
towards it.

CLAUDE

in his human shape, crawls into the
vertical service passage and climbs
up the rungs.

CLAUDE emerges from the shaft into
the dark tunnel. ANDY's nowhere in
sight. We hear only dripping water.

CLAUDE
So this is how you choose to die.
Hiding like a scared rabbit. Just
praying I don't find you...

ANDY

crouches under a concrete ledge in a very dark space. CLAUDE's voice sounds distant, echoey, and competes with the closer sound of trickling water.

          CLAUDE (cont'd- O.S.)
Well I assure you, your nervous sweat glands will give you away soon enough my trembling little rabbit.

CLAUDE

begins transforming. He falls to the ground and groans with joyous pain as his body noisily transforms.

CLAUDE (Cont'd)
AHHHH! IT'S FUCKING GLORIOUS!
AAAARRGGGHHH!!

ANDY
huddles in his hiding place, looking out into the darkness.

ANDY
(to himself)
C'mon already...

A glint of light appears in a puddle on the ground. ANDY's eyes widen.

CLAUDE

His head is transforming- his exaltations become more animalistic.

CLAUDE/beast
RRAAAAAARRRRRRGGG!!

LEDUC

still in the catacombs, hears CLAUDE's yell echo through the tunnels. He thinks it came from above. He runs towards a stairway.

THE BEAST

CLAUDE is fully transformed. He sniffs the air, locks in on a scent and sets off through the tunnel.

ANDY

watches intently as the light in the puddle gets brighter. It starts reflecting on the wet concrete walls of this tunnel.

                ANDY
            (to himself)
                Now.

ANDY clicks on the flashlight, shines it at himself, and yells for all he's worth.

                    ANDY
        HEY YOU DIRTY EVIL FUCK! C'MON AND
           GET ME! I DARE YOUR UGLY ASS!
                    (etc.)

THE BEAST

cocks its head towards ANDY's taunts. The sound of flowing water is close by. The beast pounces towards ANDY's voice, into

THE WET, SLIPPERY STAIRWAY

that ANDY slid down that FIRST night in the tunnels. The beast loses its footing and slips helplessly down the slick, eroded stone, GROWLING furiously.

LEDUC

runs down a tunnel, towards ANDY's screaming voice. The beam of his flashlight illuminates the landing ahead of him, halfway down the stairwell. He sees THE BEAST slide by, clawing in vain for a grip.

A METRO TRAIN

screams around the bend, lighting up the whole metro tunnel. ANDY is still SCREAMING from his refuge under a ledge.

THE BEAST

shoots out of the stairwell and lands on the tracks. It looks up, frozen for a split SECOND- it's horrible snarling face is caught in the speeding train's harsh glare...

SMASH!! Impact. The beast is sucked under the wheels and ground to bits between track and wheels.

LEDUC

at the landing, looks down the stairwell as the train rushes past.

ANDY

huddled next to the passing train, clenches his fist in victory.

              ANDY
              Yes!

The train passes. ANDY gets up and shines his flashlight around the ground. The beasts body lies in chunks, smears, and puddles. The parts begin morphing back into CLAUDE's human forms- A THIGH here, A PIECE OF SPINE there...

LEDUC inches his way down the last few feet of the stairway, using the rusty pipe for a handhold. He walks up with his flashlight and aims it at the BEAST'S HEAD, which finishes turning back into CLAUDE's head.

LEDUC glances at ANDY. He takes a small envelope from his pocket and shakes out a single SILVER BULLET. He loads it into his gun and FIRES straight into CLAUDE's lifeless head.

                    LEDUC
                  (to ANDY)
        I always wanted to do that. I saw
                 it in a movie.

                    ANDY
              What about me?

                    LEDUC
My men think you died and floated
away in the Seine. If I wanted to,
   I could let them believe that.
              (a long pause)
      But that would be illegal...

ANDY looks at him carefully, trying
to read him. LEDUC's face is
impassive.

cut to:

INT. COURTROOM, NIGHT

The PROSECUTOR, who speaks English
with a thick French accent, has an
extremely sarcastic look on his
face. He wheels around
dramatically, and confronts ANDY,
who sits uneasily on the stand,
wiping the sweat from his brow.

                    PROSECUTOR

You intend us to believe that you
committed these murders because the
moon was full and you were somehow
magically transformed into a huge
powerful beast with an insatiable
appetite for human flesh, is that
                     right?

                       ANDY
           You don't understand!

The PROSECUTOR turns away towards
the jury to mock ANDY.

                    PROSECUTOR
   Oh? So I don't understand? You
   think it's me who has a hard time
      coming to grips with reality?

The JURORS snigger at ANDY's
expense. But wait, suddenly they
look concerned- something's wrong.
The PROSECUTOR continues, his back
to ANDY.

PROSECUTOR (cont'd)
You think I'm the one who needs my head examined? I don't understand? Well, Mr. McDermott, enlighten me.

He wheels around to ANDY and comes face to face with

THE BEAST

huge and ravenous. It goes for his throat.

           PROSECUTOR
    Good God!!! Aaaaaaa!!!

The beast tears the PROSECUTOR apart, spraying blood everywhere. The jury - oddly enough - break into polite applause. One less lawyer...

cut to:

INT. AIRPLANE - NIGHT

ANDY wakes up with a start- a concerned STEWARDESS is leaning over him. Disturbed PASSENGERS crane their necks, peering at him like he's nuts.

              STEWARDESS
  You were screaming in your sleep,
       sir. Are you okay?

ANDY looks around, getting his bearings. He takes a deep breath and shakes it off.

              ANDY
  Yeah. It was just, um... something
       I ate.

The STEWARDESS nods and smiles, a little uneasily. He picks up the Bloody Mary from his table and gulps some down. A little bit of tomato juice dribbles down his chin. He looks out the window.

EXT. AIRPLANE

It flies along over a blanket of clouds, past the huge, silver moon. The song is Cat Stevens' "Moon shadow", sardonically covered by Nirvana, with the oh so appropriate lyrics: "If I ever lose my legs...".

ROLL CREDITS.

Printed in Great Britain
by Amazon